2006 murder connection?

death in '57

All Mortall Things

MAGGIE WHEELER

Author of *A Violent End* a ⸻ ⸻ Sleep

Published by

GENERAL STORE
PUBLISHING HOUSE

499 O'Brien Rd., Box 415, Renfrew, Ontario, Canada K7V 4A6
Telephone (613) 432-7697 or 1-800-465-6072

ISBN 978-1-897113-53-0
Printed and bound in Canada

Design, layout and printing by Custom Printers of Renfrew Ltd.
Cover photos: courtesy of Lesley, Stuart and Sean O'Gorman
Author's photo: jacqueline Milner www.jmilner.com
<http://www.jmilner.com>

The lyrics for "From Now On" and "I Know It Well" from *Retriever*
© 2004 Ron Sexsmith. Quoted courtesy of Ronboy Rhymes Inc. (SOCAN)
Sony/ATV Music publishing.

National Library of Canada Cataloguing in Publication

Wheeler, Maggie A., 1960-
    All mortall things / Maggie A. Wheeler.

ISBN 978-1-897113-53-0

    I. Title.
PS8595.H3852A64 2006   C813'.6   C2006-905856-3

Reprint February 2007

Dedication

For the men and women in uniform
who form the thin blue line that keeps us
on the right side of civilized society.

For my maternal grandmother,
Anna Gela Heipel,
an individual of great personal strength.

And, of course, for Fran,
daughter of Wales,
who kept the flame alight long before
we remembered it was a torch to pass on.

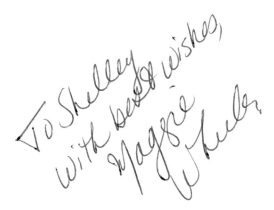

Table of Contents

Author's Note

If books took a week, rather than years, to write, they wouldn't ask so much of both reader and author. It would be wonderful if they could spring out of our heads fully grown like Athena, sword held high. But they don't, and from the first they take on lives of their own that insist on time and space in our own lives.

If you want to write (or read) books with meat in them and not be satisfied with potato-chip stories, it takes time to feel them, live them and then share them. It takes part of us.

The spark for *All Mortall Things* ignited in me at the same time as *The Brother of Sleep*, and, I must confess, the first stirrings of the final novel in the series, *On a Darkling Plain*. I have since given birth to *The Brother of Sleep* and now feel *On a Darkling Plain* slowly moving like an unborn child in my subconscious, ready for its own creation. Each book, including *A Violent End*, has demanded a piece of living I wasn't aware I needed to do and then wasn't sure I could handle. Fortunately for me, the first two times these realizations came after the novel was done.

I wasn't so fortunate with *All Mortall Things*.

Creative work of any kind is not only an expression of the human experience but also, necessarily, the next step in that experience. Each novel as it was born gave birth to new windows of thought and doorways of opportunity, all becoming successive generations of the same journey.

But first there was another journey to be taken, a devastation to be endured, a person to be found amongst the ashes. And, although I must admit I tried many times, for me there was no turning back.

The challenge here lies not only in capturing that journey to selfhood in words but also to wring it from the heart of a man. And not just any man, but Inspector Jerry Strauss—the thorn in my side for the past six years. My father was an Ontario Provincial Police officer for over thirty years. When he died in 1980, he was detachment commander in Long Sault. This is the position that Jerry holds in the series. I guess it doesn't take a rocket scientist to realize that a significant part of my character comes from the late Staff Sergeant Harold Wheeler. But even more comes from the page, from the journey Jerry started with Farran in *A Violent End*. I planned a cameo appearance for the inspector; he opted to stick around. Thus the thorn in my side.

I recently bought my own Seaway house in Ingleside—once a farmhouse in Dickinson's Landing, now sitting on a Hydro cinder block foundation of half a century. The houses of our lives maintain and change simultaneously. I sit here in the living room of my little Seaway home, looking through windows that once were graced with the vistas of Dickinson's Landing and the old St. Lawrence River. The rooms hold decades of living and dying, whispers of voices from the past. I listen and learn as I write another story from the Old Front.

And as I once again create and present lives on paper, I also begin the second half of my own.

Maggie Wheeler
Misselthwaite Cottage, Ingleside
May 16, 2006

Author's Timeout

"Out of Time" might be a better title for this note.

For the sake of clarity and out of respect for the intelligence of my readers, I need to address a small temporal problem that has developed in this series. The novels are running on one timeline, stretching from two years ago when Farran Mackenzie first set foot in the Seaway Valley to find out the truth about her father's murder. However, time in the real world has kept its own pace and it is now five years since that moment.

In Farran's world, time must work with the real history while allowing for the author's personal, much slower speed in telling her story. *A Violent End* happened vaguely around the year 2000 and was published in 2001. *The Brother of Sleep* took place in the summer of 2003 and made the bookshelves in 2004. *All Mortall Things* is more vague, but happening the summer of 2006, to be released in the fall of the same year. By the time *On a Darkling Plain* is finished for 2008, the series will have covered a fictional timeline of about four years in the characters' lives while covering a true time span of almost eight.

Where does this leave our inspector? Well, in this book he is currently grappling with the looming Big Six-Oh in his life and what it means for him. In reality, if Jerry were fourteen when the Seaway and Power Project were finished in 1958, he would have been born in 1944 and now be about sixty-two years old.

I know many of you will sense this discrepancy as you go through the novel, and I want you to understand the source of it. I guess I'm asking for a continued "willing temporary suspension of disbelief" as we make our way through another tale from the Old Front.

Maggie Wheeler
August 2006

Foreword

by Rosemary Rutley
AUTHOR, *Voices From the Lost Villages*

Wales, like most small villages, possessed its own set of dark rumours: scandals whispered over teacups on summer verandahs, or debated over a game of cards in the back room of the barber shop. They served as intriguing topics of conversation around the Quebec heaters of the villages' general stores on wintry nights—chilling tales that spanned the years, their interpretations gaining momentum with each generation. These stories and the ghosts born of them are, in essence, history thinly veiled as rumour, gossip and folklore.

All Mortall Things takes those of us who remember the pre-Seaway days on a journey into the past one more time. We walk the old Wales road again, splash in the cool, ofttimes murky, waters of Hoople's Creek, and look on once more from a deserted platform as the old Moccasin pulls away for the last time. Those who don't remember are offered a gripping mystery and a peek into yesterday, as surely all of us have known at one time or another an Audrey Beckett, a Daniel Sterling or a Jerry Strauss. The history, deftly woven into *All Mortall Things*, is seamless.

The Rice House, or the Nightingale House as we know it today and on which the novel's Sterling House is based, will never be quite the same for me. When I next enjoy a Victorian Tea there I will expect to find copy of Dante's *Inferno* on the table in the sitting room, and I will certainly check for blood stains near the fireplace. And maybe catch a glimpse of Mildred Keeps.

Like Maggie Wheeler's first two mysteries, *A Violent End* and *The Brother of Sleep*, her third combines fact with fiction so well that those who avoid reading historical fiction will enjoy the experience without knowing what hit them. Best of all, this novel leaves us with enough loose ends to keep us guessing while we wait for the next one.

When I published *Voices From the Lost Villages* in 1998, several in-depth accounts had already been written describing the engineering feat of the St. Lawrence Seaway and Power

Project. No writers, however, had explored the social and emotional issues surrounding the residents' traumatic move to the two replacement towns. No one had examined the effect of this move on those who were forced to start over, leaving behind homes that had been in their families for generations.

Voices From the Lost Villages documents life as it was in these small riverside towns before their permanent upheaval. Where once the story was penned as non-fiction, it is fast becoming a changing genre, lending itself well to historical fiction and finding its way into novels such as the Farran MacKenzie mystery series.

Together, Maggie and I have presented the story to many audiences. Historical societies, library clubs, classroom students, volunteer and church groups—all have been captivated by this fascinating piece of history.

In 2008, the Seaway towns of Ingleside and Long Sault will celebrate their fiftieth birthday, along with their refashioned cousins Morrisburg and Iroquois. Although their heritage is buried deep in Lake St. Lawrence, authors such as Maggie Wheeler will keep their story alive. Like the title of this novel, it will transcend "all mortall things."

PART ONE

What man that sees the ever-whirling wheele
Of Change, the which all mortall things doth sway,
But that thereby doth find, and plainly feele,
How Mutability in them doth play
Her cruell sports, to many mens decay?

—Edmund Spenser, "Two Cantos of Mutabilitie," 1609

Chapter 1: Love

JULY 1957

The house stood facing the Wales Road, nestled between the Beckett farm to the north and a small gully to the south that cradled Stuart Creek when it lived briefly in the spring. An impressive edifice that whispered family money, the Sterling home had been the largest in Wales and now housed the last surviving member of a once flourishing family. A large California maple—the only tree left standing in Wales—filled the front lawn with shade while the huge leaves of an exuberant Dutchman's pipe vine embraced the side porch. A concrete block wall girdled the property on the front and south sides, providing both stature and safety from the steep banks of the gully. Four concrete urns along the sidewalk to the front door had once spoken welcome with flowers, but they, like the windows, were now silent and empty, reminders of promise unfulfilled.

Although Wales itself was almost completely gone, the village grapevine was still healthy. Word had gotten out somehow that the police car now heading carefully down the old Wales Road through the new cemetery would be coming that day and would stop to pick up one passenger. One by one, the families had gathered where they once had lived and again filled the empty village street with more caution than curiosity.

Beryl Beauregard Bradshaw stood as she always had, off to one side. Silent, the former war bride shook her head from time to time as though unable to accept the tragedy that had brought them all here. She did not acknowledge her husband only a few feet away.

Rowdy Bradshaw shot the occasional glance at his wife, keeping his hands shoved down in his pockets. He did not dare to look behind him.

Beauregard "Buck" Bradshaw stood between his parents, just a little behind them. He scratched a circle in the dirt with his toe, looking up only to search impatiently to the north for any sign of the patrol car. Finally, the boy saw what he was waiting for.

"Hey, Pa!" He pushed through his parents to the front of the crowd. "Here it comes!"

Beryl tried to pull him back and hush her son, but he took no notice.

Audrey Beckett stood well back from the crowd, at the back. She had come out of the old farmhouse just to the north, the only one left on the road with the Sterling house. She wore a black dress and heels that were covered in dust from the hot wind that stung their eyes with no trees left to offer relief from the hot sun. Audrey looked at no one and spoke not a word to her former neighbours.

Jake Holmes held his daughter Lynnie's hand. They weren't from the village of Wales, having lived in Farran's Point, but knew Daniel Sterling through his father's love of horse racing. As a boy, Jake had often spent afternoons with Daniel in Dickinson's Landing or Mille Roches at the private racetracks, watching their fathers place friendly bets on the farmers' horses. Daniel had been so different then, but so had life for them all. Now, Jake guessed, he probably wouldn't know the man at all on the street. Everyone had worn a new soul when the war had ended, but Daniel had also worn a new face.

"Is this the right thing, Pa?" Lynn looked up at her father. He was the one person who always knew the answer. But this time, the man shook his head.

"There is no right thing this time, Lynnie," Jake said gravely. "The police have their job to do, but this just doesn't seem fair. And," he added, "I don't believe it somehow." He squeezed her hand and she squeezed back. The girl turned back to the house and looked for her schoolmate. But there was no sign of Jerry Strauss.

In the house, Emme Strauss stood at the front window of the old porch. She peeked through a crack in the curtains, then let them fall together.

"You should have listened to me, Daniel," she said in the faint German accent that still lingered after fifteen years, turning to the man sitting behind her. "You should have left yesterday. No one would have helped them find you."

The night before, her son Jerry had answered a knock to find a man who would not give his name.

"Give Sterling a message," he'd said, staying on the steps where it was dark. "Word is they're comin' for him tomorrow. Tell him that. Tell him," he'd continued to the boy, "that some of us think that maybe he shouldn't be here when they come. Maybe he should just head out tonight and not come back."

Jerry had told Daniel and then Emme, but the woman had been unable to convince Sterling to go.

The man in the chair did not answer for a moment. Then he smiled a crooked smile and shook his head.

"No, Emme," he replied softly. "There's no good in runnin'. I ran once before and look what it got me."

She put a hand on his arm. The sound of a car pulling up came to their ears and he stood up.

"Where is Jerry?" Emme whispered anxiously, looking through the doorway into the front hall.

Daniel put a hand out.

"Leave the boy be. He doesn't want to see me now and I don't blame him."

"But . . . "

A knock came at the door. They looked at each other and she took his hand. Daniel smiled, kissed the hand with his misshapen lips and then opened the door. This time, a young Ontario Provincial Police officer stood there, hat in hand.

"Mr. Daniel Sterling?" He studied the man's face without flinching. "I'm sorry, sir, but you'll have to come with me."

Daniel held out his wrists, but the officer shook his head.

"No, sir. For you, I don't believe it's necessary."

In the road, Jake Holmes approached the patrol car where a second officer sat in the driver's seat.

"John," he said quietly, "do we really have to do this? Daniel Sterling's a vet and a war hero. He's disfigured now. He lost everything and his best friend took his girl. Hasn't he given enough?"

The officer took off his hat and wiped his brow. "I don't like this any more than you do, Jake," he said, putting his hat back on. "But the man's confessed to murder, and the law's the law. We got no choice."

The front porch door opened and everyone fell silent. The officer came out first. Daniel hesitated in the shadows, then walked through the doorway into the sun. A few gasps were heard in the crowd, with mutters of pity and disbelief.

Bucky Bradshaw opened his mouth to holler something about the monster, but an unaccustomed feeling of remorse swept through him. He glared at both his parents and said nothing.

Daniel had started down the steps when a boy came out of the front door and ran down to him, throwing his arms around the man. Sterling held him for a moment. No one heard what the man whispered in the boy's ear, but it seemed to be enough and the boy let him go. Then Daniel turned and, head held high, walked down the steps toward the patrol car.

Emme Strauss came out and took her son's hand. As the officer opened the back door of the car for Daniel, Jerry tried to bolt.

"Jerry, no." Emme grabbed her son and held him fast.

"I should have been here, Ma." He struggled in her grip. "He didn't want to go out to the train and I should have stayed with him."

"It's not your fault, Jurgen," she said soothingly, falling into his German name. "It's not your fault. The police will handle it."

Jerry stopped struggling and let his frustration give way to tears.

"Leave him alone!" he screamed at the officer. "He didn't kill anybody! Daniel! Tell them. Tell them it's a mistake."

Both Daniel and the officer turned back, but Daniel's reply was cut short. Audrey Beckett moved through the crowd and came up to him with a hand out.

"Daniel. . ." she began.

Sterling stepped back instinctively. The officer waved her away and Sterling looked back at Jerry, eyes blazing in the dead face. He raised a fist, then pointed at the boy.

"Remember your Shelley, son," he called out. "Shelley. Remember. That's a promise." He looked around at everyone except Audrey, and got into the back seat of the patrol car. The officer closed the door, then turned back.

"Another promise," he said, walking up the steps to where the boy still stood with his mother. "We'll take good care of your dad. Don't worry about him. And we'll make sure you can visit in a few days, okay?"

He's not my dad, Jerry wanted to say, but somehow didn't. He nodded slowly and then watched the man walk back down to the car. The officer got in and the car started up.

For just a moment, Daniel's tortured face appeared in the back window as he took one last look at his family home. Then the car began to pull away.

Everyone was silent, watching it take the rise to the new No. 2 highway with its lone passenger.

As with the archetype Harper Lee would soon create, Boo Radley had come out.

Chapter 2: Fear

INGLESIDE 5:30 A.M.

The house stands at the corner of Maxwell Avenue and Santa Cruz Drive, its half-shuttered windows keeping sleepy-eyed vigilance on Ingleside. Peaks, gables and closed-in porches rise above the rooflines to its south, the historic building visible in profile all the way to drivers on County Road 2 along the St. Lawrence River, proclaiming the refuge promised on the blue and white highway tourism marker: Sterling House Bed and Breakfast.

"Supper," muttered Mildred Keeps. Wrapped in a floral housecoat, the petite middle-aged widow began the breakfast routine she could do in her sleep. "All had to have supper last night," she told the kitchen gruffly in her clipped British accent, being diminutive only in size, not in sound. "And all in their rooms." She grabbed the shrieking kettle off the burner, flipped the switch on the coffee machine and took a quick look out the window.

Dawn. Sun just coming out. Mildred longed to head out to her gardens. The best way to enjoy such a beautiful late spring day. The Victorian gardens that surrounded the old house on its double lot were at their first peak of the season and she still had many more plants standing like Beefeaters all around her office, waiting for their roots to kiss the earth.

"Think I'll get a minute today?" Mildred asked herself, an ongoing conversation born of years lived alone. "Seriously doubt that," she responded. "Not with the royal tour in town and a full house because of it."

And *she* was here.

Four guests, including the one person who held Mildred in thrall. Should never have started going to the casino out of boredom. Debt. And the legal right to take it all away.

How would she cope? Where would she go?

And her uncle? Well, it would just kill the old man.

"Uncle Hugh?"

Mildred carefully pushed open the door to the room at the top of the stairs. In its day, it had been the nursery. Now the small room housed the oldest occupant in the bed and breakfast. Her uncle, Hugh Keeps.

Putting the tea tray beside the bed, Mildred pulled the drapes open and looked down at the old face on the pillow. Strange, wasn't it, how at even such an age, a person can look so childlike when sleeping. Yet her uncle would be well over ninety by now.

She turned away. Had to keep this from him as much as possible. When she'd gone to bed last night, Mildred had found Hugh wandering in the corridor and steered him back to bed. He was upset about something and she hoped it wasn't about Sterling House.

"Want my tea, Millie."

The woman turned back to find the elderly man half sitting. God love him, she thought with genuine affection. Hugh was a handful at times to be sure, but if it hadn't been for him, five years ago she would have been alone again.

"Pillows, Millie," Hugh ordered with the unnecessary volume of the hearing-impaired.

"Yes, Uncle." Mildred patiently punched and plumped, then propped him up. When she handed him the tea mug, he grabbed her free hand and held it tightly.

"I saw her again." Despite the trembling chin, the old man's eyes were clear—and held the first trace of fear she had ever seen in them. "She's not supposed to be here. Something's wrong."

"Who?"

"The girl."

"There is no girl here, Uncle Hugh." Sitting down on the bed, she patted his hand. "Only adults. We don't take children, remember?"

"I saw her," he snapped back. "The same one as last week. There's someone here who is not supposed to be here. We have to find her."

Mildred sighed. The story of Sterling House being haunted had lingered since its days in Wales. At the time she'd bought the house, it had seemed fun and fanciful to play it up in promotions. But right now she wasn't so sure it had been a good idea. At least Hugh wasn't on to the threat of losing the house.

"Drink your tea," she said in her best bedside manner. Still came natural, even after years of retirement from nursing. "I'll be back. I have to get dressed and wake the guests. It's almost six o'clock." She rose to leave.

The old man seemed mollified and leaned back on the pillows without further comment. But his voice suddenly caught Mildred at the door.

"Don't worry about the house, Millie," he said sharply. Surprised, she turned to look him in the eyes. "I'll take care of things," he continued. "You won't lose this house. Not to anyone."

The Nursery was one of four guest rooms upstairs. The first bedroom with its door facing the top of the stairs was the Blue Room, so named after its colour scheme and shady atmosphere, despite the large window overlooking the gardens. Beside the Nursery just before the turn in the hallway was the Gold Room, a little larger than the Blue and more formal in its gold-tinged decor which was lit daily by sun from windows facing east and south.

After the turn in the hall, another short hallway with built-in bookshelves on either side branched off to the left, leading to a small sitting room. Once an open porch, the sitting room was bright and sunny, full of windows, plants, chairs and books for the guests' leisure time.

The hallway then continued past a little table on the left, right beside the door to the largest guest room—the Brass Room. Given its name because of the large brass bed inside, the Brass Room was the brightest of them all, as well as the largest, due to windows in a small, private sitting room that backed onto the other in the hall. It even had a window that offered a view of the main sitting room as a reminder of that room's beginnings as a porch.

Across the hall from the Brass Room was the shared four-piece bathroom. The hallway ended with the door to Mildred's room, imposingly labelled "PRIVATE."

In the Blue Room across from the nursery, Buck Bradshaw called out a thank-you for the wake-up and closed his eyes again. Damned sleep. Or lack of it. Sleep of the damned. Shouldn't have come back here. To this house. Was the job worth the trip down memory lane? Some would call it coming home. But he hadn't been home for years and didn't think it was possible. Quaint idea, but not for him.

He rubbed his eyes and sat up. Full day ahead. No rest for the weary—or the wicked. He'd make sure of that. Only a few hours left to make tracks and then the timing would be gone. Well, not gone, but certainly not what it was today. What a headline it was going to make. The big story he'd been waiting to break his entire career. It would take down another career to do it, but those were the spoils of war. And if he got a chance to lock horns with Jerry Strauss one more time, well, it would certainly add to the entertainment value.

Buck got up and admired himself in the mirror that hung over the ornate radiator in the corner of the room. Grey streaks and a little rounder than he'd like, but still had the killer dimples and smile that had been worth their weight in gold over the years with the ladies. Still were when he had to. Not bad for a guy facing sixty.

Sixty. Shit. Age didn't scare him, but time did. Time left. Got to get on with it. Time and money. He wanted both.

He would put up with the ghosts for a few days to do it.

The house hadn't really bothered him when he'd arrived last night, but looking into those eyes again right here after almost half a century had reduced him in a frightening second to a boy. The boy who couldn't hold his mother while she cried.

The man turned away from the mirror. This time he would do the right thing. He'd stumbled into this chance and he would stare it down. This time, he wouldn't look away.

Buck grabbed his bath towel and headed off to the shared bathroom to be the first one in. He paused and listened at the door of the Gold Room, but then walked quietly past the Brass Room, opposite the bathroom.

Walked quietly and looked away.

Isabella Roberts, Minister of Canadian Heritage, lay awake in her bed in the Gold Room. She had been up for an hour but remained quietly in her room. It felt as if she were hiding. Maybe she was. A hell of a long weekend going on this time. But it would be the icing on the cake of her career. A legacy to accomplish before retiring to the corporate world and all its monetary benefits.

If things didn't go AWOL right now.

She'd mastered chess at ten, romance at fifteen and Parliament by thirty. No one was going to shake her down when everything was in the balance. No one gets the upper hand on Bella. Not for long, anyway.

After all these years, she needed help. And the only person who could help her was the one person whom she knew never wanted to see her again.

She heard someone walk past and go into the bathroom.

"I'm next," Isabella announced grimly to the room and threw back the covers. Time to start the show.

And remember what Dad had always said. Any piece on the chessboard is expendable to save the king.

Any one.

Mildred was brushing her teeth in her private bathroom when she first heard the shouting.

"Dead! Dead! Call 911!"

Someone pounded on her door. Full of serious misgiving, Mildred opened it. Stanley North, one of the couple in the Brass Room, stood there in his pyjamas, hair as wild as his eyes.

"It's Audrey!" he shouted. "She's dead. Somebody's killed her."

Thinking fondly of the duct tape in her kitchen drawer, Mildred tried to hush him. She could hear the shower running in the bathroom. Hopefully, it would mask the conversation.

"Calm down, Stan. Audrey probably just took an extra sleeping pill last night and didn't tell you." She took the man by the arm and led him to the open door of his room.

Audrey North lay on the bed, eyes and mouth open, a knife protruding from her chest. Mildred put her hand to her own mouth and walked up to the bed. It didn't take her nurse's training to see that Stan was right. Audrey was very dead.

"Oh, God," Mildred whispered, closing her eyes as if to brace herself. Not now. Not *now*.

She went back into the hall, where Stanley stood looking at the hallway that led to the sitting room.

"Stan. Stan."

He seemed to come back from very far away.

"*Stan*." Mildred grabbed him and shook him. "You're right. Audrey's been killed. You have to come and sit downstairs. I'm locking the room until I can get the police in here."

"Why do we need the police?" Stanley's voice was absolutely flat.

"What's happened?" They turned to see Isabella standing in the hallway at the corner.

The door to the washroom opened and Buck came out, clothes on one arm, towel wrapped around his waist. He didn't bother to blush.

"A lineup," he grinned. "Sorry. I didn't think I took that long . . ." His voice trailed off as he took in the scene over Mildred's shoulder. "What the hell . . .?"

Mildred snapped into action, locking the bedroom door and then her own with her master key. She pushed through the guests to head downstairs. Hugh Keeps stood in the doorway of his room with a stricken look on his face. He put out a hand to stop her.

"Millie," he said softly.

Mildred looked at him for just a moment and touched his face gently. Then she marched down the main staircase, out through the closed-in front porch and out the front door. Without slowing down, the woman hurried across the street to the unmarked police car parked on Maxwell.

Lynn Holmes sat in her car on Santa Cruz, listening to the top-forty morning show on her favourite Ottawa station. Clad in her usual jeans and T-shirt, with unruly brown curls that even middle age would not tame, she kept a quiet eye on the street. The village seemed deserted, with streets and sidewalks bare except for one car on Maxwell with someone waiting in it. She hoped it wasn't another journalist.

But it was another beautiful spring day. And the weather even looked good for the entire weekend, which should help out with the festivities. Unusual that the weather should co-operate. Maybe it was a good omen for the minister's tour and announcement about her plans for the Seaway Valley.

"So here I sit in wait for a pre-interview like a rookie on her first assignment," she muttered. More than three decades of journalism, an editorial post with the *Ottawa Citizen*, and she'd parked at dawn to wait out the minister for an exclusive. But this was personal. This was home.

Did she even have a home anymore? She'd kept herself carefully at arm's length from this community for years, and now that Meredith was gone, there were no family ties left. But she had been born and raised here. Or at least out there. Lynn turned to look at the sunrise coming up over the river. Out there under the water were the last traces of the village of Farran's Point. And her childhood.

Being homeless was one of the bonds between herself and Professor Farran Mackenzie. The stranger who had come home for the first time that terrible summer of Meredith's death to deal with a violent end in her own life was a kindred soul and probably the only close friend she had besides Ruth Hoffman. Lynn and Farran had both chosen to pursue their professions to the exclusion of marriage and family. Both had been very successful. And now both were middle-aged and alone. Technically speaking.

Farran, at least, had had a daughter in her youth that she was now trying to find. Lynn had helped her dig around for contact for the last six months since Farran had moved here permanently. Even though they'd faced one dead end after another, it was only a matter of time before they scored a hit. And Farran had formed a relationship with Jerry Strauss. An uneasy alliance sometimes, but a relationship nonetheless.

"More than I've managed to do," Lynn said, snapping the radio off. More than she'd actually tried to do. It wasn't only the community she'd kept at arm's length all these years. Many good men, too. And now she was counting down to sixty. Retirement loomed.

Sixty. Shit. Where the hell did the time go?

Lynn suddenly sat up as the front door to the Sterling House B&B burst open and a little woman with a brilliant housecoat went steaming down the sidewalk and across the street to the car parked on Maxwell. After a brief but intense conversation with hands flying, the woman went back into the house followed by the occupant of the car—a female Ontario Provincial Police officer in full uniform.

The front door slammed shut. Peace and tranquillity reclaimed the empty streets. Lynn hesitated only a moment.

"So much for good omens," she said, and swung open the car door.

Inspector Jerry Strauss, OPP, lay across his bed in full uniform, eyes closed. If he weren't careful, he would fall asleep that way. Might feel good at the moment, but experience had taught him that leather belts and holsters hurt the body after a few hours.

At least get the boots off, he thought drowsily.

Getting damned old, Strauss. An eighteen-hour shift wouldn't have laid you low like this ten years ago. Thank God he didn't have to do them that often. But an overturned fuel tanker on the 401 with four dead and a spill across both directions of highway had scrambled what few officers he had to spare with everyone in place for the minister's tour. There was no bugging out for his favourite chair and the new DVD collection of Abbott and Costello that waited for him at home. Not till the sun came up and everything was secured. He'd sent Wiley home to sleep for a few hours and now it was his turn. Had to be coherent in time for the banquet tonight.

Not that he even remotely wanted to go.

Strauss pulled himself off the bed and made his way to the bathroom, leaving a trail of OPP parts along the floor in his wake.

Isabella Roberts. Minister of Canadian Heritage. Did not want to go there at all. A VIP tour, the likes of which Jerry hadn't seen in the Seaway Valley since the Queen went through in '59 to open the Seaway. Even his picture in the *Ottawa Citizen* as the one personally requested by the minister's office to supervise security. All this public profile stuff was wear and tear. He preferred the old days when the only people he had to stroke were lawyers and criminals.

He looked into the bathroom mirror at the face that stared back. Tall, dark, greying. Women had always called him handsome. But almost sixty. Shit. Body creaks and a cataract in one eye. His mother had died at sixty from cancer. He seemed to spend more time thinking about the past these days than the future. Like taking early retirement. But what the hell would it mean? He'd chosen career over family his whole adult life, except for one close call. And what works in professional life rarely pays off in personal. No children. No grandchildren. Not even a significant other to make plans with.

Except Farran Mackenzie. Strauss picked up the watch lying on the counter that she'd left from her last visit there.

Don't know what you'd call the relationship he had with the woman. In many ways, they were kindred spirits. Both homeless by choice and by events. Both loners by trade. Yet somehow he always ended up being with her, mercurial though she was by nature.

And with Farran blowing into his life, unearthing her father's murderer one year and stumbling into the unsolved death in Mille Roches the next, it felt as thought the past was coming back with a vengeance. There were mornings he'd look out the glass doors of the detachment in Long Sault at the river and half expect to see the Lost Villages rising from their watery graves.

Farran had called him her best friend last fall, even after the terrible mistake he'd made that had cost a life. It didn't help much what she'd revealed to him. It was still his fault. Maybe that's why he needed to take early retirement despite Farran's best efforts to talk him out—

The phone by the bed rang and he went out in his boxers to answer it. When he heard Detective Sergeant Wiley's voice, Strauss instinctively sat down on the mattress. Not good.

"Sir." Wiley's voice was full of apology even before he said the words, and Strauss cut him off.

"I know it's important, Wiley. What's up?"

He heard the officer clear his throat.

"We have a 10-45, sir. Constable Taylor just called it in."

"A 10-45?" Strauss stood up. A 10-45 was a dead person. "Taylor's on watch at the B&B."

"Yes, sir. One of the guests didn't wake up this morning, and the owner came out to get her."

"Who?" The sandwich from the vending machine that had served as breakfast suddenly turned to lead pellets in his guts.

"Don't know yet, sir. Taylor called in from the car. All she knew was that the owner said it was a woman."

A woman. Strauss closed his eyes. I'm not a praying man, God, but please don't let it be Isabella Roberts.

"I'm on my way. Meet me there," Strauss ordered.

"Sir, you haven't had any sleep," Wiley protested. "Couldn't I—"

"I appreciate the offer, Wiley, but I have to be in on this." He couldn't screw up again, especially with this. "We have a federal minister in that house and a dead woman. God help us if they're one and the same. Even if not, we have a hell of a situation on our hands."

He thought for a moment.

"Listen, Wiley. This is between us for now. You, me and Taylor, until I say different. Use an unmarked car and wear your civilian dress. I want the situation and location wired shut until we need to open it. Not even any Mounties until we have to. The last thing we need this weekend with everything going on is a media circus in Ingleside."

He hung up and sat down again, fighting the urge to lie back on the bed.

Isabella Roberts.

MP.

Sterling House again after all these years.

And no sleep.

Well, he wasn't tired now, Strauss thought grimly. Nope. Not tired at all.

He'd just graduated to goddamn numb.

And somewhere in the old house, the girl stood listening in the dark.

"Something is wrong," she whispered over her shoulder. "We have to stay here. You can't be seen."

Turning to look at the person behind her, the girl slowly shook her head.

"You cannot leave right now. I will keep you safe.

"It's death," she added softly. "Death has come to the house again."

PART TWO

Have we been blind
Have we been lied to
Best keep our eyes open
From now on
There's no peace of mind
When the war's inside you
It feels like something's broken
Something's gone

—Ron Sexsmith, "From Now On"

Chapter 3: Interregnum One

HALIFAX, NOVA SCOTIA
6:00 a.m. EST / 7:00 a.m. AST

Time is not linear. Ask anyone who works with it, such as a history prof like me, and we will tell you it is brutally circular. Spock once told Kirk that time is, in fact, much like a river with currents and eddies that wash us back to certain points in time again and again. And for just a moment that early morning, I felt that I was drowning in the past. Again.

I sat in the airport café in Halifax, Nova Scotia. Waiting. Waiting for a friend to come back with coffee. Waiting for answers to questions I wasn't sure needed answers. Waiting to go home to my new life in the Seaway Valley. Waiting for my heart to admit that I deeply gave a damn about someone other than myself for the first time in a lifetime.

And waiting until the last minute to leave the brief limbo I had enjoyed for the past few months since the winter of my discontent, the emotional sick leave I had cashed in after a bomb had torn a hole in my life and my heart.

Just like years ago.

Another May morning, 1982. The coffee shop in Gatwick airport, England. A twenty-four-year-old incarnation of Farran Mackenzie, newly pregnant and—even more dangerous—deeply in love with an older, married man. A woman-child driven by passion and despair to consider crossing the line between humanity and hell. Almost. A woman who sat for fifteen minutes in a seat on transatlantic Flight 39, thinking she could allow one life to end so that her own and one unborn could have what wasn't theirs. And then she had bolted—out of the airplane, past the stewards who called out after her, past the roped-off area and into the crowd. Into the coffee shop. Into the brief limbo between one life and another.

I sat doodling on my notebook in Halifax, watching the planes leave the tarmac and head into the Atlantic sunrise. I remembered that young woman who had been me, sitting, shaken, at a table, unable to even get a coffee for my nerves. Trying to rationalize the irrational, telling myself that it wasn't my decision. But it was. And the woman who could not stand up to get a coffee had finally walked out to the pay phones and dialled Scotland Yard.

"I think he's going to kill her," I had whispered. I had given names, and an address. Then hung up. One lifetime over. One door closed forever.

I don't remember how long I stayed in the coffee shop after I returned. I had made one coffee last a second lifetime, long enough to be still there when the news came in. When people starting talking and gathering around the flight timetable screens, when I followed suit and heard how Flight 39 had ended in a fireball over the Atlantic. How all the right people in England would soon think I was dead. How the next lifetime had begun for Farran Mackenzie.

And that Farran had disappeared. From the airport. From Gatwick. From England. From herself. Even, eventually, from her own child.

"I think the question is not how, but why. Why children?"

An old friend and former colleague, Samson Doyle, set two coffees on the table in front of me and sat down. Like his predecessor, Doyle had prodigious locks that flowed to his shoulders—albeit with the first streaks of grey. Still, after all these years, my fingers itched in their presence and I jammed my hands in my pockets.

"Okay, then," I said. "Why children, Sam?"

He shrugged and the locks quivered. "I don't know, Farran. Could be like the poltergeist phenomenon and tied in with the energies of the children who see them. Sometimes children only feel comfortable appearing to children."

"That's possible," I replied, "but the other factor is that the sightings are happening only in houses moved during the Seaway construction. That must mean something."

"I take it these are the older houses in the villages?"

I nodded. "But there are some original homes scattered in the outlying areas that don't seem to be affected."

"You're the history prof, Mackenzie," he grinned. "I'm just the ghostbuster. Refresh my memory about the Seaway."

Sam was a lot more than just a ghostbuster. We'd done our undergrads at York University and then parted ways for graduate degrees on opposite sides of the world. I pursued my love of factual history while he was lured into the murkier side of the past—myth, legend, lore. Ghosts. Parapsychology is the modern term. Samson Doyle was one of the first to take on the relatively new field of paranormal research and was largely responsible for the credibility it now has in Canada. As far as ghostbusters go, Sam was top dog.

"From 1954 to 1958, the federal governments of Canada and the United States worked together to construct the St. Lawrence Seaway and Power Project." I relaxed into my professor mode knowing I had an appreciative audience—unlike the glazed eyes I often got from Jerry Strauss. "Technically, it runs from Beauharnois Lock in Montreal to the Welland Canal in Ontario. It opened the St. Lawrence River up to international shipping traffic for the first time by replacing the old canal system built in the last century. It also created a huge power dam complex that still fires up over two million watts of energy every day for Ontario, Quebec and Upper New York state." I took a sip of my coffee. "But to do that," I continued, "almost nine thousand people on both sides of the river had to be relocated when their land was expropriated. On the Canadian side, eight villages were affected—six of them vanished forever. Where I come from, we call them the Lost Villages."

"And some of the homes made it into your village of Ingleside?"

"Yes. Ingleside is one of two towns created to house the people from the six villages. It was a massive undertaking. Counting the houses in all eight villages, over five hundred buildings were relocated in three years."

"And now suddenly, there is a rash of sightings in the moved homes?"

"That's what Diana says." Diana Wiley is Detective Sergeant Jordan Wiley's teenage daughter. The first time I had blown into town with all the best intentions, stirring up a mess of trouble, we had struck up an unlikely friendship. When it was over and I was homebound and healing from my brush with death, Diana had started visiting to keep me company. We found we shared a passion for history, especially the local one.

Last fall, Diana had approached me about something all the kids were talking about in school.

"Fan, can I ask you something?" Diana looked pensive. "I've been wanting to talk to you privately about it. I . . . I don't really know who else to ask."

I looked at her face and braced myself for a life issue, hopefully not one that would be her mother Michelle's strict domain.

"Sure. Fire away."

Diana hedged for a minute, fussing with the china.

"Do you believe in ghosts?" she blurted out.

"Ghosts?" I echoed. Now that was one I didn't see coming.

"Yes, ghosts. I mean, well, with all the history work you do and old places you hang out in I thought . . . I thought you'd be the person to ask. Do ghosts exist?"

I unwrapped the old teapot and held it for a moment.

"If you had asked me that question even two years ago, I'd have said no. I've spent my adult life approaching history with the intent to capture the reality of it. Myths and legends are fine, but only as clues as to what the people were thinking and feeling at the time." I stopped.

"But," Diana prompted.

"But then I came here." I set the teapot down. "The Seaway Valley is the cradle of Upper Canada. They might have rearranged things here fifty years ago, but that fact remains. It's a very old part of the country, even going back beyond that with the native Mohawk and the Iroquois." I looked at Diana. "I've heard the voices from the Lost Villages."

"The ones that are supposed to come from the river?"

I nodded. "It's happened more than once. One time, it saved my life. I don't know why I hear them. Maybe it's as simple as I'm willing to listen. Now," I added, "why do you ask?"

"Well, I've been hearing about things from my friends."

"Things?"

"Things that are happening in some of the old houses. Things they see."

"Such as?"

"Children," came the unexpected reply.

"Well, well, well." Sam crossed his arms and smiled. "Farran Mackenzie believing in ghosts. After all the arguments we've had over the years. I'm glad you're telling me face to face. Otherwise, I'd never believe it." He looked pointedly at the book I had brought for the trip, *A Return to Love*. "Marianne Williamson," he noted. "That's a bit spiritual for you, isn't it? What's up, Mackenzie? Growing a soul in middle age?"

I had both the grace to blush and the wisdom to keep my mouth shut. Sam grinned at me.

"Just razzing you as usual, Mack. But I'll warn you about Williamson," he added sincerely. "She's tough. She'll back you into a corner and make you choose between love and fear."

I did not reply.

"What's this about voices from the Lost Villages?" Sam changed the subject.

"It's a local legend," I explained. "The story goes that the villagers were so unhappy about losing their land that after death their spirits returned to the sites of their former homes, and at night if the wind is right, you can hear the voices coming across the river where the villages used to be."

At this point I usually got at least a shiver. Sam didn't bat an eye.

"And you've heard them?"

I looked deeply into my coffee.

Run.

Run, child, run.

Danger. Go.

I closed my eyes.

The flames. The smoke. The fear.

This way, Fan . . . the window is this way . . .

I opened my eyes and looked up at Sam.

"Yes, I have." I thought for a moment. "And more than once, Sam, they saved my life."

"So, obviously, the voices are beneficent. And it sounds as though they are active and not just imprints."

"Imprints?"

Sam nodded. "What we call psychic imprints. Residue of a person left behind that repeats the actions he or she did in life. Some of the voices would qualify, I guess, if all they do is speak across the water. But others, like the ones you've heard, are active and like the traditional ghost we talk about or see in the movies.

"If the children are imprints," he continued, "all you have to do is change the surroundings in the houses significantly to get rid of them. But active ghosts are different. And don't ask for anything weird like an exorcism," he added, putting up his hand. "I leave that for mediums and the like. And there is never any guarantee that it will work. If these young spirits aren't really bothering anyone, why do it?"

"What could you do?"

"Mostly just ascertain that the visitations are real. I'd bring infrared cameras, digital remote thermometers to register sudden cold spots, or an EMF meter."

"Speak English, Sam." I gave him the Spock eyebrow. "EMF is . . ."

"Electromagnetic field. The meter registers strong EMF activity in a building. If there are no electrical appliances nearby, it could indicate a psychic door opening and closing, causing the sighting."

I set my paper cup down on the table. "I'd just like to know what it all means."

"Then I'm going to suggest something very unscientific." He sat back in his chair, lacing his fingers through his hair. My fingers twitched again and they were promptly returned to my pockets. "Approach this living myth through your heart, not your head. When did the sightings begin?"

"More or less in the summer of 2004. Fifty years after the Seaway construction began."

"And it has continued and even accelerated since then?"

"That's what the kids say."

"Then, Fan, if it's true and the sightings are real, two things come to mind. One, the children from the past have a message to pass on. And two, the children in your village today have to listen."

We both fell silent, taking in the import of that statement.

Listen? To what? A warning?

My cell phone rang and I jumped. I flipped it open like Kirk's communicator and answered, hearing a voice I knew yet did not recognize.

Michelle Wiley, wife of Detective Sergeant Jordan Wiley, mother of Diana Wiley. Teacher, community force of nature, Martha Stewart district commander and—thank God—a good friend of mine. Smart, resilient and tough as nails.

This voice did not belong to that woman.

"Fan. It's Diana . . . where did she go? We can't find her."

"Michelle, calm down. What do you mean, where did she go?"

"She disappeared last night . . . April says she's hunting ghosts, Fan. I know you two are working on something about that. Where did she go?" Her voice rose in panic.

"She's hunting ghosts?" I saw Sam sit up in his chair. "Who is April?"

I fought to keep the panic out of my own voice. "Michelle, take a breath and start from the beginning."

I heard her pause and knew she was pulling in her strength. When Michelle spoke again, it was much more the woman I knew.

"Diana went to a sleepover last night at her friend April's house. I was to pick her up today after lunch. I got a call from April's mother just now and they are both in hysterics. Diana snuck out of the house last night at sundown and was going to stake out a house that is supposed to have a ghost. April covered for her, but finally fell asleep waiting up. When she woke up this morning and Diana hadn't returned," the voice quavered for a moment, "April told her mother and they called me." That must have been a horrific moment for April's mother, I thought. Michelle added, "I didn't want to call Jordan just yet, in case this was just a teenage prank." I heard her take a deep breath and let it out. "Fan, do you know anything about this? Do you know where she is?"

I wanted so much to say yes. I wanted to know that within the hour, Diana Wiley would be safe in her bedroom, grounded for the rest of her life. I looked at my watch and calculated, allowing for the time difference. Possibly ten hours since she left April's. The coffee began to bounce in my stomach.

"No, Michelle." I said quietly. "We never discussed doing anything like that. It must be a plan she came up with on her own. I don't know why she would. But let's not panic until we have to. Diana's too smart to do anything really stupid. She probably just fell asleep wherever she went and she'll show up soon totally embarrassed."

There was silence at the other end. Neither one of us believed it.

"Jordan is working," came the reply. "Out on a call. Overtime. They're strapped to the limit for the weekend."

"Let's do some groundwork then, before we panic. Then we'll call the police. Get April on the phone to everyone she can think of who might know where Diana is." I hesitated. "Michelle," I began slowly, "do you think Diana might be with Ryan?"

I heard Michelle sigh. Ryan was Diana's first real boyfriend— and the thorn in her father Jordan's side. In the past month, the usually close father and daughter had had some real fights about Ryan and he was, to be diplomatic, a touchy subject in the Wiley household.

"You know, Farran, that's really why I hesitate to call Jordan. It's very possible. Maybe that's why April is saying she went out to hunt ghosts." Michelle was silent for a moment. "Farran," she added finally, "as much as I'll be mad as hell if it's true, that's exactly where I hope Diana is because at least she'd be alright."

"Everything will be alright, Michelle," I said more to myself as a prayer, eyes closed. "I'll be landing in Ottawa around 9:00 a.m. I'll check in as soon as I get off the plane. Make the calls, and let's not panic until we have to."

Michelle hung up, the panic in her voice hanging in my ear. A mother's love. A mother's fear.

A choice between love and fear, Sam said. I had ritually chosen fear, as my mother did before me. Fear, not love, in getting involved with a married man. Fear, not courage, in Gatwick. Fear, not love, in giving my baby away. But sometimes we have to deal with both. Sometimes we have no choice. I loved Diana Wiley like my own daughter. And fear for her was growing like a Chinese buffet in my stomach.

I slapped the phone shut and answered Sam's gaze.

"Do ghosts ever kidnap people?" I asked.

Chapter 4: Ghosts

INGLESIDE 6:00 a.m.

"Even the birdcage," Strauss muttered, unbelievingly. "Even the goddamn birdcage."

"Sir?" Wiley asked.

They were standing in the front closed porch of Sterling House, Strauss at a dead stop in the centre, Wiley waiting uncertainly on the threshold. Strauss had hesitated only a second before walking into the old sitting room, but it had been a second too long. The past had come rushing up at him, as though half a century had never passed.

. . . This will be good for my son. He is lost without his father . . .

Remember your Shelley, son . . .

Leave him alone . . . he didn't kill anybody . . .

His mother's hand on his shoulder.

It is not your fault, Jurgen. The police will handle it . . .

It was 1957 again. The chairs set to face the windows, the pictures on the side tables, the plants everywhere. Even the birdcage open and empty. Uncanny how the new owner had reproduced the old sitting room, where he had spent so many nights that summer listening to Daniel Sterling's stories. But this was clean, polished and inviting, not at all like the indifference he'd walked into in Wales that first morning.

FLOOD DAMAGE STAGGERING
Audrey Hits Ontario; Many Dead In U.S.
2000 Stood Watch Near Toronto

TORONTO (CP)—Hurricane Audrey, enfeebled by a Louisiana campaign and the long march north, messed up the Southern Ontario landscape but civil authorities said the storm aftermath didn't look too serious.

Historic House Moved On Cannonball Express

History recently rolled out of the past and into the future . . . all with the aid of a trio of cannon balls. The story concerns the moving of the famous old Robertson house from Maple Grove to the site of the proposed Crysler Memorial Village being erected by the St. Lawrence Parks Commission near Crysler's farm. The house is one of the most historic in the Seaway Valley. It was built about 145 years ago at Maple Grove near Mille Roches by Arthur Robertson, great-grandfather of Miss Lottie Robertson from whom the house was recently purchased.

Saturday, June 29, 1957
The Cornwall *Standard Freeholder*

"You wait in the porch, Jerry." His mother was in her Sunday best, with white gloves and hat. The widow, married young to Jerry's father, was still only in her thirties, still beautiful with white blonde hair wrapped in its customary French twist. They stood in the dusty road outside the large house with the glassed-in front porch. It spoke of a better time, more people, more money. But now the house was quiet as though empty, windows shuttered, gardens overgrown. Yet his mother was acting as though they were going to meet the queen. Emme Strauss smoothed her dress, walked up the few steps from the road to the front sidewalk and opened the door without knocking. Jerry followed her into the porch and took the chaise she indicated without a word. Again the woman did not knock, but opened the main door and entered the house.

The boy looked through the dirty windows at the neighbourhood around him—or what was left of it, which wasn't much. Wales was almost empty now, the Sterling house sitting alone on the hill as if in defiance of the devastation all around it. The huge Hartshorne moving machines had been hauling houses from the old villages into the new towns now for over two years. The Hydro workers had been cutting trees since the first word went out about the deep-water project actually going to happen after fifty years of talk. What wasn't moved was destroyed—burned or bulldozed into the ground. He'd watched with a child's interest as people left their family homes, moving into a new bungalow in the new towns, coming back to watch Hydro burn their former homes to the ground.

And then wishing they hadn't. Pretty soon, Jerry had stopped watching, too.

The voices murmured on inside the house. The late June day was hot, the porch even hotter. No respite even after the storms. Restless, he wandered out onto the front lawn and found refuge in the shade of a large California maple.

"Hey! Hey, kid!"

Jerry looked around to find the speaker, also a kid, a boy about his own age, standing at the end of the driveway. When Jerry beckoned him over, the boy shook his head and hooked his thumb towards the road.

"I never go near that house," said the boy when Jerry joined him. "If ya ever go in, you'll never come out. Everybody knows that. I'm Buck. Bucky Bradshaw. I live down the road, or at least I used to. What are you doin' here?" He crossed his arms and tried to look down at Jerry, though they were the same height. Curly brown hair, old dungarees, bare feet and a fishing rod over one shoulder. Jerry, in the slacks and clean shirt his mother had made him wear this morning, eyed the stranger enviously.

"I'm gonna be stayin' here for the summer, to work around the house and help Mr. Sterling get ready to move."

Buck's eyes opened wide.

"You can't mean you're goin' to stay with the monster? He'll kill ya and cut your body up in parts."

"The monster?" Jerry willed himself to not look over his shoulder at the house.

"Yeah. Sterling's the last of the family left. Came back from the war with a bunch of medals and no face. My dad says he got it burnt off savin' someone's life. His girl took one look at his face when he came home and left him. Now he sits in there alone every day and never comes out. My dad says he's crazy. Even chased the Hydro guys away when they tried to cut down that tree." Buck gave a nod to the California maple. "Made the papers an' all." The boy looked pointedly at the house. "Is that lady in there your ma? I wouldn't leave her alone in there too long if I was you . . ."

In spite of himself, Jerry was already across the yard. He took the four steps in two strides, ran through the porch and burst through the front door.

" . . . This will be good for my son. He is lost without his father . . ."

His mother sat on a divan in the living room, speaking to someone out of Jerry's line of sight. When she saw her son standing in the hallway, breathless, Emme slowly rose in concern.

"Jerry?"

"Sir?" Wiley repeated.

"The police will handle it," Jerry muttered, and pushed open the front door. He stood in the hallway, the swing door to the dining room facing him, the stairs to the second floor on his right, the archway to the living room with its ornate wooden columns on his left. He didn't waste a moment getting his bearings. After almost fifty years, he still could have walked through the Sterling house with a blindfold on.

Constable Margaret Taylor stood in the living room. Strauss watched the tall, slim brunette through the peepholes the columns offered at eye level. She was writing something in a notebook in her hand. A woman sat on the Victorian divan behind her. Middle-aged, grey hair, violent housecoat, pink mules on her feet. Decidedly unhappy, unless a grim line was the best smile she could do. Hands clasped quietly in her lap, yet sitting bolt upright as if ready to run. Nervous. But then, sudden death had that effect on people sometimes.

Strauss switched his focus to Taylor, joining her in the living room.

"Okay, Taylor. You're first officer on the scene. Let Wiley have the bottom line and we'll get started."

"Yes, sir. Mrs. Keeps, this is Inspector Strauss and Detective Sergeant Wiley. Inspector, this is Mildred Keeps, the owner of Sterling House. She has four guests upstairs including the deceased," Taylor glanced at her notebook, "a Mrs. Audrey North. Mrs. North was discovered dead in bed this morning by her husband Stanley North, who then alerted Mrs. Keeps."

Strauss felt his shoulders go down an inch. It wasn't Isabella Roberts.

"Alerted?" The woman on the divan spoke without looking up. "Brought the house down. Had everyone in an uproar first thing in the morning. Excitement like that isn't good for my uncle. He's very frail for his age."

"Your uncle is staying here right now, Mrs. Keeps?" asked Wiley.

"Her uncle lives here, Sergeant," Taylor supplied. "He occupies one of the upstairs rooms. Hugh Keeps."

"Where is everyone?" Strauss looked around the room and into the dining room.

"My uncle is in his room with the door closed," Mildred spoke up. "I don't want him disturbed. It will be too much excitement for him."

"The other guests are in their rooms, waiting. The minister requested privacy until you got here, and I thought it best to corral Mr. Bradshaw for the minister's sake until Sergeant Wiley arrived. And Mr. North, of course," Taylor added. "He's lying down on the couch in the TV room just off the dining room. Mrs. Keeps says she gave him a sedative."

"I gave him a stiff shot of brandy. The man's a mess, of course." Mildred still did not meet Jerry's eyes. "Do I start breakfast?" She finally looked up, but at Wiley who had come in to stand behind Strauss. "Everybody will be hollering for breakfast soon, and my uncle needs regular meals for his diabetes."

"Yes, go ahead, Mrs. Keeps." Strauss fixed his gaze on her, waiting for eye contact. Odd. "Life goes on for the living. But," he added to Taylor over his shoulder, "the guests will have breakfast and stay in their rooms for now, until we can speak with each of them. No one goes out. And," he finally turned to her, "ask them nicely for their cell phones. All chit-chat is off for the time being. We're going to keep this absolutely quiet and hold off on the media circus as long as we can. Mrs. Keeps, are there phones in the rooms?"

She shook her head. "No. Only mine. Not that it would do them any good this morning. The line's dead."

The house was as dead inside as it was out. Jerry stood in a room full of old furniture, curtains closed against the morning sun, walls and tabletops bare of pictures of any kind. Instead, there were books. Probably close to a hundred. On tables, in piles on the floor, even some taking up the chair seats. Everything covered in a thick layer of dust—except the books.

"Jerry," his mother said reprovingly, "I asked you to wait outside."

"He's here now," a male voice cut in. "Let's have a look at you, boy."

The speaker stood as Jerry slowly walked over. The man was tall, well over six feet, and carried himself with a military stance. Unlike the room, he was immaculately dressed, every detail church-perfect—except for his face. There wasn't one to speak of. The other boy was right. It was gone, or at least partly erased as though it had melted in the summer heat.

But the eyes held a piercing intelligence.

"Come closer and take a better look, boy. My face is the best the air force surgeons could do after the fire. If you're bunking here for the summer, you'd better get used to it."

Jerry hesitated, then walked up and looked him right in the face. He saw a brief flash of approval in Sterling's eyes. "It happened when you saved someone's life, right? Are you a hero, Mr. Sterling?"

The man's mouth became a thin line.

"I'm no hero, boy. I just saved the life of a . . . a friend." His eyes softened and the thin line became a very crooked smile. "And it's not Mr. Sterling. Looks like I'll be trippin' over you all summer. Best call me Daniel. But don't let that fool you. I'll be workin' you hard. I've dug my heels in for three years, but the house has to be moved this summer. I'm out of time. We have a lot to do before then. This is a big house."

"It's a big house."

"It's a beautiful old home," Wiley agreed and Jerry started, not realizing he'd spoken out loud. They were alone in the living room. Mildred had headed for the kitchen to start breakfast, Taylor upstairs to confiscate cell phones. Strauss looked around the room, eyeing the Victorian decor approvingly. Keeps had done a great job of restoring the vintage beauty of the house and, as with the front porch, had pretty much nailed it as to how the house had looked in 1957. Except, of course, the housekeeping. Strauss took in the dining room beyond the archway. Even the silver tea set sparkled.

"This house came from Wales. The Sterling family built it in two stages, starting in 1880. It was the largest frame home moved during the construction of the Seaway. Daniel Sterling ended up with a double lot for no extra charge because the house was so big it legally sat too close to the property line on its single lot." He grunted. "An extra lot he never got to use."

"Why not?"

"The house made it to Ingleside. Daniel Sterling didn't." Strauss looked at a key in his hand, the one Mildred Keeps had given to him before grumbling off to the kitchen. "Like I said, it's a big house. It's going to be a job to keep things nailed down for the next few hours. Upstairs, four bedrooms and a bathroom. Main floor is foyer, living room, dining room, den, storage room, kitchen. Now an attached two-car garage out back. And I assume the house is sitting on a large cinder block basement courtesy of Ontario Hydro. I don't want anyone off by themselves today until further notice. After I see the body, we'll have a chat with everyone one at a time. We keep everyone together and babysit them at all times. We'll need one room to work in, maybe the den after we deal with Mr. North. Now let's go see who didn't wake up this morning."

All the rooms were in the same state of neglect. Daniel Sterling took them through the house, telling Emme Strauss more than Jerry what had to be done with things. Boxes to be gone through, closets emptied, trash thrown out. The old cellar cleared out completely.

"Not that I need to because of the house moving, I guess," Daniel said, leading them out the back door to the yard. "I hear the Hartshorne people have you leave everything the way it is, even lamps on tables. Nothing moves inside. Sounds too good to be true."

"It's not, sir—Daniel." Jerry trotted beside him, a little breathless. "I've watched them move a dozen homes, and they're gonna move my friend Hal's to the museum village . . ." The boy's voice trailed off for a moment, a dark look crossing his face. Daniel glanced at him, then up at Emme. She imperceptibly shook her head. "It's really something," Jerry continued. "The tires on that mover are as big as a man. And they put this lifter thing through holes under the house and up it goes as quiet as anything."

They stood in the backyard, overlooking the little ravine that ran along the south side of the property. It had been fenced off to keep little Sterlings from tumbling down its banks. Just down a bit next to the fence stood a large barn-like structure with a substantial garden also fenced in right beside. Unlike the house, the garden was well-tended. A long garage occupied the other corner of the yard. The north side of the property shared a fence with a neighbouring farm that, like the Sterling house, was still intact.

"These buildings aren't coming, of course," said Daniel. "And the Sterlings have never thrown anything away. I have to get rid of everything. Sell it all, I guess. Sell the building for scrap, too." He looked down at Jerry. "How old are you, boy?"

"Thirteen."

Sterling nodded. "My dad built that garage when I was about your age. We built it together. Now I got to tear it down. But better me than some strangers coming to burn it down. It's been terrible on some folks to watch their houses go up in flames, I hear."

"Who are your friends, Daniel?"

At the sound of a woman's voice, Emme and Jerry turned to see her standing on the other side of the fence. Daniel instinctively turned away. Jerry saw his mother put a hand on the man's arm, but he did not turn around.

"That's her, Emme," he said so low Jerry could barely catch it. "That's Audrey."

Without a glance backward, Daniel Sterling went back inside the house.

In the Brass Room, Audrey North lay on her back, knife protruding from her chest.

Strauss and Wiley had walked quietly up the stairs to the second floor, ignoring any faces that peered out from the guest rooms. Blue Room at the top of the stairs, door open a crack. Nursery across the hall, door closed tight. Constable Taylor was tangling with the woman in the Gold Room next to the Nursery, whose voice could be heard before they reached the top stair.

"I can't be without my cell, officer. My people need to reach me twenty-four/seven, especially today."

Jerry had felt his shoulders rise, but he'd squared them and walked past the doorway without a glance.

"I'm sorry, Minister Roberts." Taylor's voice flowed over the protest. "This is a crime scene now and we have our protocol . . ."

Around the corner, past a short hallway that led to a small sitting room. Then the Brass Room on the left, the bathroom on the right, and a door at the end of the hall that said "Private." Once a storage room. Now Mildred Keeps' room, Strauss surmised. It was locked.

Wiley unlocked the door to the Brass Room and let it swing open, remaining in the hall. Both officers took in the room without entering. Bedroom with an attached sitting room. A window into the other sitting room in the hall that had once been an open porch like the front entrance. Victorian vanity, two nightstands, large bed with brass headboard and the dead woman in the middle. There was a smell of death and blood in the air, and something else. Jerry sniffed carefully, then shook his head. Violets? But it was already gone. A quick glance at the vanity table didn't help. Mrs. North used Chanel No. 5.

"Start the backgrounds with Mrs. North," Jerry told Wiley, then carefully walked over to the bed. One knife, protruding from the chest. A single stab wound to the heart. Death would have been instantaneous. The knife had a long, ornate handle, and Jerry felt the flicker of an old memory. Then he bent down to look at the dead face—and felt the floor tilt suddenly.

That face. Even in death, even after fifty years, even under a spill of faded auburn curls he knew that face.

Sterling House. Violets. Audrey Beckett.

"Audrey?" he whispered to himself.

That's her . . . That's Audrey. . .

The eyes were open wide, as if death had been a horrid surprise. He remembered those eyes—as cold alive in the past as they now were in death.

He had put it all away for half a century. All finished and done with. And now it was back. All coming back. For him. For what?

For one crazy second, Jerry had to fight the urge to turn and look through the window to the street below. If he did, it wouldn't be there. It would be Wales again, the farms, the decimated properties, the constant trucks, the Moccasin screaming past on the Grand Trunk on its way to Montreal. He'd heard about things like this. Time warps. It was crazy. It was science fiction. It was . . .

"It's my goddamn lack of sleep," he growled to himself as he stood up.

"Sir?"

"I met this woman a long time ago." Jerry met the question in the sergeant's eyes. "Her name then was Audrey Beckett. She was born a Connelly. Lived in the village of Wales until they tore it apart. She was important to someone important to me."

There were voices on the stairs, one stern, one flippant. And footsteps running up.

"I'll find the inspector, thanks."

"Hey, you! You can't go up there! I said wait down here!"

Mildred Keeps, Jerry thought. And . . . no, it can't be. He backed out of the room, signalled Wiley to lock the door and headed to the landing to head off . . .

Lynn Holmes stood at the top of the stairs, in front of the door to the Blue Room. Mildred Keeps was on her heels.

"Ah, Inspector," Lynn smiled dangerously. "I have a few questions for you."

"Lynnie, what the hell . . ." Strauss snapped.

The door to the Gold Room burst open, a middle-aged blonde woman in a power suit sweeping out into the hall with Constable Taylor right behind. The former came right up to Jerry and opened her mouth to speak. Taylor stepped in between them, putting her back to the stairs.

"Minister, I really think with Mr. Bradshaw here . . ."

Strauss heard Wiley come up behind him. Millie moved in front of the Nursery Room door and stood with her back to it.

"Taylor," said Strauss, keeping his eyes from meeting those of the Minister of Canadian Heritage, "what's the concern with this Bradshaw?"

As if on cue, the Blue Room door swung open. Buck Bradshaw stood there. He locked eyes with Strauss and walked out, a slow smile creasing his face.

"Well, well, well. If it isn't Jerry Strauss. You don't look happy to see me," he said sarcastically. "I thought absence makes the heart grow fonder. Well, I'm happy to see you. And what's all this? I keep walking into parties in the hall around here."

When no one answered, Bradshaw took them all in, lingering on Lynn, then focusing on Strauss again.

"Wow," he said with a laugh. "You, me, Lynn, this old house—and Audrey cooling in the next room." A grin broke out across his face. "Just like old home week, ain't it, Jurgen?"

Chapter 5: All Men's Decay

INGLESIDE 7:00 a.m.

In the half century Lynn Holmes had known Jerry Strauss, she had never seen him speechless. But at that moment, for almost a full minute, he did not say a word.

Starting with Bradshaw, Strauss looked at everyone on the landing as though seeing each for the first time. All were as silent as he, like recruits at their first inspection. When Strauss got to Wiley, he looked over the man's shoulder to the locked door down the hall. Finally, he turned back to the waiting group.

"Mrs. Keeps," he said quietly, speaking in the dead calm that had a history of causing ulcers in police subordinates, "please continue with breakfast downstairs. And coffee," he added pleasantly. "I'll need lots of that."

Mildred turned to go, checked the door to the Nursery Room was locked, and disappeared down the stairs.

"Taylor," Strauss continued, "take Minister Roberts back to her room and keep her there until I call for you. Sit on her if you have to."

As Taylor moved to obey, Isabella Roberts faced Jerry. "Inspector," she began sternly.

Strauss looked her right in the eyes. They struggled for a moment, but something in Jerry's eyes had the desired effect. Roberts set her lips into a fine line and turned back to her room. Check, Bella, thought Strauss. Let's see who gets to say checkmate. Taylor raised her eyebrows to him and followed, locking the door behind her. As she did, Bradshaw moved forward with Lynn on his heels.

"Minister Roberts," he called out.

Strauss put up an arm to intercept him.

"I think not, Mr. Bradshaw," he said evenly. "You will stay in your room as well, until I need you. Detective Sergeant Wiley has a lot of questions for you, Buck. As a matter of fact, so do I—as you can imagine. So," Strauss locked eyes with the man, "you can answer them here, or . . . you can answer them at the detachment. And it may take us a few hours to get back to you down there."

Buck opened his mouth to speak and closed it again. He sighed, crossed his arms over his chest and grinned.

"Any time you're ready, Strauss," he challenged, and vanished into the room.

Strauss looked at the closed door thoughtfully for a moment, then turned to Lynn.

"Wiley," he said over his shoulder, "carry on. I'll escort the media out of here."

"Hey," Lynn protested as he took her by the arm, "Bradshaw is media, too. If he stays, I stay."

"Bradshaw is a guest." Strauss ignored her plea and started herding her down the stairs.

"And what did he mean about someone named Audrey 'cooling off' in another room? Has something happened?"

They reached the front hall and Strauss opened the door to the porch.

"No comment as usual. Go home. I have a long day with the minister's visit—"

"Hey." Lynn stopped dead in the middle of the porch. "This is weird."

Strauss opened the outside door. "When you and I are in the same place, it's always weird."

"No," she insisted as he led her through the door, "the porch. I didn't notice when I came in . . ."

"Why *did* you come in?" Jerry came to a grim halt on the front sidewalk. If he believed in omens, this wouldn't be good. Press inside the house, press coming through the goddamn door. "What the hell are you doing here, anyway?"

"I could ask you the same thing," she replied pointedly. "I can see having your officer here for security, but the Big Cheese himself?"

"Answer my question, Holmes."

There was a warning in his voice Lynn knew well enough not to ignore. She pointed to her car on Santa Cruz.

"I came early to stake out the minister, get an exclusive before the press conference this morning."

"I can guarantee no interview this morning. Besides, I thought your street days were over, Jimmy Olsen."

"Usually, but not if something special is going on. Have you heard from Farran since she left?" Lynn changed the subject. "I haven't had a call and it's been a week."

"Just once when she arrived in Halifax," Jerry said shortly. "Nothing since then." He shrugged and began to lead her in the direction of her car. "I assume she's chasing that ghostbuster."

Or Paul Vaughn. The name rose in his mind and he squashed it. Jealousy was an emotion he never permitted. It had cost him too dearly in the past.

"I should call her," said Lynn. "I have some news for her."

"You do that. From *home*." They reached her car and Jerry opened the driver's door. "Go home or go to Cornwall, have breakfast and get a good seat for the conference. Just don't stay here. I don't want to have to take you to Long Sault with Bradshaw."

Lynn stood looking at him. "Jerry," she said slowly, "What Buck said upstairs. About old home week . . . and Audrey." Strauss looked away and she put a hand on his arm. "He didn't mean *that* Audrey, did he?"

When Strauss didn't answer, she tightened her grip.

"Jerry," she whispered, "what the hell is going on in that old house?"

Stanley North lay stretched out on the couch in the small den just off the dining room. At Strauss and Wiley's entrance, he opened his eyes and slowly sat up. Still in his pyjamas, black hair up like a newborn bird, the man was small and wiry with inexplicably large hands he kept curled into fists.

Strauss stuck out his own.

"Mr. North, Inspector Strauss. SD&G OPP. My detective sergeant, Jordan Wiley. Our deepest condolences on the loss of your wife. Do you feel up to answering some questions?"

North shook hands and nodded. Strauss noticed he seemed a little woozy. Death and brandy are a tough mix. He wondered if Stan had snuck a few extra shots once alone, but didn't see any bottles in the room.

Strauss took a chair, indicating to Wiley to do the same.

"I take it you found her dead this morning when you woke up?" he gently asked Stan.

North nodded again, looking at the floor. "I had my back to her. I turned and she was there with that thing in her chest . . ." The big hands shook and the fists curled tighter.

Strauss looked at Wiley.

"Mr. North," said the latter, "did you see or hear anything in the night?"

"No, no . . . I take sleeping pills for insomnia so when they hit, I'm out."

"And your wife seemed fine before you went to sleep last night?"

"Yes. She was reading when I turned out my light."

"How long have you been here, Mr. North?"

"Uh, let's see . . ." Stan rubbed his eyes. "This is Saturday, right?" He looked at Wiley who gave him a quick nod. "We got here Thursday night. We're leaving tomorrow." He stopped while it sank in. "I . . . I guess not, now."

"Are you here for business or holiday?"

"Both. We live in Toronto. Really like it down here. But Audrey had business. She always did."

"And what would that have been?" Wiley led him carefully, letting the man get his brain back in his head.

"Don't know. Never kept tabs on what Audrey did." Stan shrugged. "Just stayed close and drove her around. That's how we met, actually. I was her chauffeur and bodyguard years ago. She decided I did such a good job that she married me. And I did do a good job taking care of her all these years. Until now, I guess."

"Mr. North, we don't know who killed your wife or why she died, but we will," Jerry said. "I'm sure this has been quite a shock to you. I smell coffee and I think you need food, too."

"Clothes, sir," Wiley muttered.

"Uh . . . right. Wiley will open the room and help you get some clothes for the day, Mr. North. It's going to be a long one."

Stan stood up and moved toward the door. Then he stopped and turned to face Strauss.

"I loved my wife, Inspector. If you don't get someone's head on a platter for this, I will. And I don't care how high up they are," he added ominously.

Strauss rose and towered over the little man. Bodyguard? Must have special training.

"I understand your grief, Mr. North. But also understand I have an investigation underway here. Do not, I repeat, do not do anything to jeopardize that. Does anyone here have reason to want your wife dead?"

The question seemed to clear Stan's head for a moment.

"Audrey didn't make her money by being nice to people," he said dryly. "She was a tough businesswoman. But to kill her?" He hesitated for a moment, then shrugged. "Like I said, Inspector. I didn't keep tabs."

Wiley followed North out.

The smell of coffee came back at Strauss through the swing door and he closed his eyes. Stifling a yawn, he pulled out the business card Lynn had given him earlier outside Sterling House.

"I need your card," he'd answered cryptically to her question. "With your cell phone number on it. And Lynnie," he'd added, reverting to her childhood name, "get out of here, but don't go too far. Stay close. I may need you."

She'd handed him one without a word, then got in her car and drove off. As he'd walked back to the house, Jerry had automatically looked up at the second-storey windows.

And watched a curtain be hastily pulled shut. The Nursery Room.

"This will be your room," Daniel said, stopping at the top of the stairs. He opened a door to his left to reveal a small room with a window looking front to the road. A single, freshly made bed on one wall faced an old dresser on the other. A tiny closet held linens. Unlike the rest of the house, this room was immaculate.

Also unlike the rest of the house, pictures adorned the walls. Pictures of children from over the years in prams, sitting with dogs probably long dead, or posing with flowers now dust. One frame sat on the dresser alone, displaying the beautiful smile of a blonde girl just a few years younger than Jerry.

When the boy picked up the frame to look at her, Daniel nodded.

"That's my aunt, Harriet Sterling. Pretty little thing, wasn't she?" The man looked at the picture over Jerry's shoulder. "The photograph was taken just a few months before she died."

"She died?" Jerry echoed.

"Yep." Daniel moved away to put Jerry's duffle bag on the bed. "Just ten years old and the apple of her daddy's eye. She fell into the gully when it had water in it and drowned. They put the fence up then, but it was too late for Harriet. My grandparents were never the same. Life, son, is a symphony of joy and despair."

He looked up at the boy, his eyes courting a twinkle.

"They say she haunts the house. You can tell by the violets, the flower she was picking when she fell. That's the flower she loved, son. Legend says that scent follows her spirit in the house." He turned away. "Never ran into it myself."

Ghosts.

Later that night as Jerry tried to sleep in the strange bed, he looked at the picture in the moonlight and wondered if he believed in ghosts. He did make sure the closet door was closed.

A truck drove by on the road below and it reminded him of all the times he'd ridden with his dad in the lumberyard truck. Those days were gone, as gone as the lumberyard that had burnt to the ground with his father in the office. After the fire and the funeral, Jerry had often tiptoed in to the front room, half expecting to see his pa sitting there in pants, shirt and suspenders, reading the paper as he'd always done.

But nothing. No father, no ghost, not even a feel of his presence. Bill Strauss had walked out the front door and was never coming back.

Jerry Strauss sat in the den, listening to the sun. He had a brief moment of peace while waiting for Wiley, and he tried to wrap his mind around the murder of Audrey North. But the brain fog from his fatigue quietly rolled in and he found himself being taken back half a century to that summer he had worked so hard to forget.

The weeks with Daniel Sterling and their conclusion would have been enough for a boy of thirteen. But coming on the heels of his father's death and in the turmoil of the Seaway construction tearing apart the only world he'd ever known, it had been a defining summer in his life.

Another promise, the police officer had said the day they took Daniel away. And he'd kept his promise. When Daniel refused visits in jail, the officer had come to see Jerry personally to tell him and explain. He hadn't just walked away like the others. For the life of him, Strauss couldn't now remember the man's name. But he did remember choosing to be like him, to be there, to not walk away, to eventually wear the uniform of the Ontario Provincial Police.

Bill Strauss had died, a suicide that still lay unprocessed in the heart of his adult son. And Daniel had confessed to murder and disappeared into the justice system. Hal . . .

But with Hal Leonard, it had been different.

Didn't you leave Hal before he left you? whispered the guilt in his heart. *Didn't you believe what they said about him? Your friend?*

"No . . ." Strauss muttered, his forehead furrowed as though in pain.

What do you think Farran thinks of that? You let her father down.

"I didn't mean it," he shook his head slowly. "I didn't know . . ."

Then Jerry felt a hand on his arm. Looking up, he saw Hal Leonard standing there, young, alive, grinning that lop-sided grin he'd always had.

"Hal?" he whispered. "You're here. Was it all a mistake?"

Jer, it's okay. Strauss heard the voice; yet Hal did not seem to open his mouth to speak. *It's okay . . . It wasn't your fault.*

Hal moved away toward a door.

"Hal," Jerry tried to rise but his legs felt like lead. "Hal, I'm sorry. I should never have believed them. I should have made you stay."

Hal turned back for a moment.

You were just a kid, Jer. It wasn't up to you. He seemed to put out his hand. *We'll always be friends . . .*

The door swung open and he vanished.

The door to the den swung open and Strauss's eyes followed suit. A tall, fair-haired late thirty-something, Wiley stood in front of his superior officer with a notebook.

"Is everything okay, sir?"

"Yes," Jerry said uncertainly. "Everything's fine." He gave a cautious glance around the den. There was no one else there. "Where do we stand?" he said rubbing his eyes, turning back to the sergeant.

"Stan North is having breakfast," said Wiley, once the door had closed. "Amazing he can eat with the morning wake-up he had. Not to mention having to get his clothes around his wife with a knife in her chest, even under the sheet."

Strauss grunted. "Something tells me that wouldn't bother someone like him. Bodyguard. A little man like that. Wonder what his background is."

"I can call in for that now, plus the others," Wiley offered.

"Wait on that. Wiley," Strauss rubbed the gravel in his eyes, "you're the detective sergeant. This is your investigation. I'm only here because of our federal minister and her request for my supervision of her visit. But," he added, "she *is* here. As is Bradshaw, right down the hall. He's the biggest mouth in Eastern Ontario. We have to walk carefully with this one. So, consider me the front man for the morning. Everything will run through me, be my responsibility. You have your entire career ahead of you. I'm applying for early retirement. As far as the suits in Toronto are concerned, I'm bulletproof. You're not."

"Do you think it could be that bad?"

Strauss didn't answer for a moment.

"There's something else you should know," he said finally. "Something's not right here. It's . . . it's weird." He grasped onto Lynn's word.

"You mean other than the body upstairs?"

For any other officer, that would have earned The Look. But Strauss knew sarcasm was not in Wiley's policy manual.

"I told you upstairs that I knew the dead woman long ago." Strauss hesitated. "This is personal—and off the record, Jordan." He looked at Wiley, whose head snapped up at the unprecedented use of his first name. "In 1957, I stayed in this house in Wales. Just for the summer. I was to help Daniel Sterling pack up four generations of family history and move the house to the new town of Ingleside. Audrey North was Audrey Beckett back then, married to the man who had been Sterling's best friend his whole life. Problem was, Audrey had first been engaged to Sterling and her marrying Beckett had ended the friendship between the two men. That summer, Beckett was murdered. Stabbed in the chest in this house. I found him. Shortly after, they took Sterling away for the murder after his confession and I went home. He was sentenced to hang. His war record and his disfigurement from service was taken into consideration, and they commuted his sentence to life imprisonment. I never saw him again. Two years ago, after Farran Mackenzie showed up and dug up all those old ghosts, I decided to track him down." Strauss stopped.

"He would be an old man by now," Wiley offered. "Do you think he's involved with this?"

"No." Strauss shook his head slowly. "I'd waited too long to find him. Daniel Sterling had been paroled and was living in Southern Ontario. He died about five years ago of pneumonia in Hamilton Henderson General. He was in his seventies and alone. He'd be over eighty by now."

You walked away from him, too, Strauss, thought Jerry.

"But," Wiley continued to connect the dots, "you wonder if this murder has anything to do with that. Right?"

"Maybe I'm more tired than I think, Wiley, but the back of my neck is telling me to at least think about it. Like I said, something's not right here. Something's . . . well . . . weird. Not just why is Audrey dead," he stood up and stretched, "but why is she even *here*? Here in the house where her husband died violently so long ago. And Bradshaw, too."

"He's media, sir. And tabloid stuff most of the time. The worst kind. He's obviously here to tag the minister."

"Bradshaw grew up in Wales," Strauss replied shortly. "They had moved his house before that summer, but he was still around. Just a kid, but there. And now he's here. *Here*. Just like Audrey, except no knife in the chest."

"Not that there wouldn't be a long line of volunteers with his track record," Wiley finished.

Strauss was quiet.

"Sir," Wiley ventured, "this is my case. What can I do for you? What do you need here?"

"Time." Half a century of it, he thought sadly. "I need time. Not much. Just a couple of hours, tops. Wait to call ident. I don't want a flurry of uniforms in here and outside. Let's say it's to protect the minister until the banquet tonight. Turn off your cell phone and all calls will go through me. Taylor should have all the cells by now, and Keeps said the house line was out. Let's look into that.

"We'll stall just long enough for some questioning," he continued. "I just need to get the feel of this situation before it's disturbed." *Feel.* Did he say that? Facts and procedure had been his whole career. Still, policing was an inhuman job done by people for people. The human factor was the difficulty—and the whole point. Dammit, Farran. Where are you when I need you? This would be your home turf.

As if reading his thoughts, Wiley said, "I think Farran Mackenzie would say that what you need to do is to listen to this old house."

That got him The Look.

"Coffee, sir?" Wiley smiled.

Strauss grunted. "And an office."

Mildred Keeps, still in her housecoat, set a plate of steaming eggs and sausage in front of Stan North at the dining room table, who was now dressed and brushed.

Jerry came out of the den and looked at Mildred.

"Mrs. Keeps?"

She jumped.

"*Millie!*" came a bellow from above.

"That's my uncle. I'm sure he's quite upset." Mildred buzzed past Strauss without a glance.

"Mrs. Keeps," he repeated. She stopped reluctantly. "Can you unlock the door to your office in the den? I need somewhere private to interview your guests."

"*Millie!*" came a second bellow. Mildred turned, glared at Strauss and went into the den.

Well, thought Strauss, at least we've made eye contact. That's a step forward.

Strauss followed Mildred with Wiley on his heels.

The office was a small, narrow room off the den that ran alongside the house. It had been an open porch initially, and then closed in to make a sitting room on the south side of the house when in Wales. Daniel Sterling had used the room for storage, with piles of boxes almost to the ceiling laced with dust and cobwebs.

Jerry half expected to see it looking still the same as the other rooms did, but Mildred swung the door open on a neat office with desk, computer, file cabinets—and plants. About twenty large potted plants and two dozen little ones filled the room, blooming in the southern exposure. A jungle, thought Strauss grimly. Wonder if there are bugs. He still hated bugs.

"Wow," said Wiley.

"Do what you have to," Millie snapped, "but don't hurt any of my plants. They were to go out this weekend and now this." She turned to leave.

Wiley walked over to a tall, leafy presence in the corner. "Is this a fig tree, Mrs. Keeps?"

She paused. "Yes, why? Is that suspicious?"

Wiley smiled his best let's-calm-the-victim-down smile. "No, no. I was just admiring it. It's so healthy. And the variegation on the leaves is very nice. The one I have at home never seems to be very energetic."

"Give it more light," Mildred said grudgingly, "and I find this brand of fertilizer helps the most." She picked a bottle off a shelf and handed it to him.

Strauss pushed forward into the office, almost tripping on a green vine trailing across the floor.

"Watch the trumpet vine," Wiley and Mildred said together.

". . . sir," Wiley added. "They're quite beautiful in bloom. Isn't that an ivy geranium?" He pointed to a potted plant that had made friends with the window blind.

"Yes. The others are the regular geraniums. They all should be outside now," Mildred muttered.

"And this?" Wiley moved over to a tall, leafy plant near the window, seemingly oblivious to the cold stare from Strauss.

"That's a brogmansia." Mildred joined him, touching the large leaves gently. "I winter it here and it leafs out somewhat before going back outside. Once outside, though, it almost doubles in size and puts out an oversized trumpet flower. They are quite hardy for this area. This one is peach and white mix."

"Wiley." Strauss shifted his weight to one foot.

"I've seen pictures of them," Wiley commented. "They look almost tropical."

"Wiley."

"I have three more upstairs." Mildred's scowl was gone and she seemed to be fighting a smile. "Perhaps I could start a cutting for you, Officer . . .?"

"*Wiley*," said Strauss for the third time.

"Officer Wiley," Mildred continued. "Do you live in Ingleside?"

"Long Sault, actually, ma'am. But that would be great. My wife loves unusual plants."

Strauss drew a deep breath, but his blast was cut short by a louder bellow from upstairs.

"*Millie! Where are you?*"

That broke up the plant party.

"Mrs. Keeps," snapped Strauss. "Go ahead and see to your uncle. We'll have questions for both of you shortly."

She shot him a glare he had to respect, then what looked like a smile at Wiley before disappearing in the direction of the yelling.

Wiley fussed with the brogmansia for a minute before meeting Strauss's steely gaze.

"Brogmansia?" The sarcasm was palpable.

"Uh, yes sir. It's becoming quite popular—"

"*Notebook*," Strauss barked. "Roberts first. Bradshaw can have breakfast with North, Taylor as referee. And get that goddamn vine away from me."

Jerry sat under the Dutchman's pipe vine on the side porch steps. He felt eyes on him and turned to see Daniel watching him from the door.

"Too hot to do any real work, yet," the man said through the screen. He looked around the yard and out to the road. *"Looks quiet here today. Let's go out back."*

Jerry hopped up and joined him in the house, following him out to the dining room. Daniel stopped in front of the sideboard and pulled a box of bullets out of its top drawer.

"That's a neat knife," said Jerry, looking at a knife with a carved handle mounted on the wall over the sideboard.

Daniel carefully took it down and handed it to the boy.

"That knife belonged to Granny Hoople."

"Granny Hoople?" Jerry turned it gingerly in his hands. The blade was not long but the handle was, carved with what looked like vines and flowers.

"The first woman doctor of Ontario," he said with a quiet pride. *"She saved the people here from starvation in 1788, the hungry year. Mary was a Whitmore, her mother a Sheets. They lived in Pennsylvania until the family was massacred by Revolutionary Indians in 1780. Only Mary, her sister Sarah and her brother John survived. For seven years, Mary was raised by a Delaware medicine woman who taught the girl all she knew. Then Mary was sold to the British for food and brought here to live with her uncle, Jacob Sheets. The timing couldn't have been better."*

"Why?"

"Because it was 1788, the second year the crops failed and famine set in. People were starving, but Mary knew from her Delaware upbringing how to find food in the forest. She also knew folk medicine from her Indian mother and began to help people. Word spread fast and Mary became known as the 'doctor woman.' She was just a girl, but she was hope to desperate people."

"And she saved everybody?" Jerry had heard some of the old story once, but wanted to know about the knife.

"Yes. If Mary hadn't come that winter, Lord only knows what would have happened to the people of the Longue Sault Rapids. She married Henry Hoople and had twelve children. All lived to be adults except one. Little Mary Hoople, the family pet. Four years old and she swallowed a hot coal from the fireplace. Must have been terrible for her mother. All the lives she saved and the one she couldn't was her own little girl. Still, Granny lived to be in her nineties, a doctor woman to the people here her whole life. The Hoople house is still up on the Second Concession."

"And this was her knife?" Jerry ran his fingers over the carved handle. It certainly was beautiful.

Daniel nodded.

"It was given to her by her Delaware mother. She used it to cut special plants for her medicines. I have it now because I'm a Hoople on my mother's side." Daniel took the knife and replaced it on the rack. "Her eldest boy was named Gerry, you know, after Henry's father Jurgen."

"That's my real name," said Jerry, "but no one uses it 'cept my ma, and that's only when she's really mad at me."

Daniel smiled his crooked smile and picked up the box of bullets, walking out to the kitchen where a long rifle leaned in one corner of the room.

"Did your pa ever teach you to shoot?"

A shadow passed over Jerry's face.

"No, sir. He . . . he had to work a lot because the Seaway made the Leonards' sawmill so busy, and then . . ."

"I'm sure he would have if he'd been able to," Daniel said quietly, handing him the bullets. "Let's go take some practice shots outside around the barn."

The man took a quick look around the yard before venturing out with Jerry on his heels.

With quick work, Daniel set up some old tin cans on the fence and then showed Jerry how to hold the rifle.

"Now the thing to remember, son, is not to fight it." Daniel took the rifle and put it to his shoulder. "It should feel like part of you, work with you. And just before you shoot, let all your breath out so you're steady." He fired off a shot and one can spun into the air. "Now you try."

Jerry took the gun, feeling its weight. He'd never held one before. His father Bill had not been a hunter, even for sport, although many of his friends' fathers were. Jerry loaded with Daniel's help, took aim and fired. Nothing moved.

"Again," said Daniel simply.

Another shot. This time a chunk of the fence below the cans flew off.

"Better." Daniel nodded, pleased. "I think you have a feel for this, son, like I do. Took to it like a fish to water. Practised all the time. And that's all it takes. Practise. Do all the shootin' you want here, Jerry. Someday, you'll be able to do this." The man took three cans and built a pyramid with a gap in the centre. Then he took a fourth can and set it behind. With ease, he loaded and *fired. The can behind disappeared. The cans in front did not move.*

"Wow," said Jerry. "Did the army teach you that? You must've killed a lot of soldiers over there."

"No. No . . . I . . ." Daniel looked away. "I was in the air force. They taught me how to fly planes. I never killed anyone." He handed the rifle to the boy and slowly walked back to the house, leaving Jerry with the rifle near the barn . . . in the hot summer sun . . . and the hazy, pleasant scent of the violets . . .

Violets.

A warning bell went off in Jerry's head and his eyes snapped open.

But the scent was gone, and his head was in his arms on the desk. Can't sleep. Can't falter. Can't screw up on this one.

He stood up suddenly and felt the blood rush to his head. Taking deep breaths, Strauss steadied himself on the windowsill. Then he heard the door open.

"Inspector?" Wiley poked his head in. "Minister Roberts is ready to be questioned."

"Fine." To avoid Wiley's look of concern, Jerry turned to face out the window. "Send her in and close the door on your way out."

Wiley opened his mouth, then closed it. He opened the door wider and stood aside, for the woman who followed.

The Honourable Isabella Roberts, PC, MP, Minister of Canadian Heritage, swept in as though the bell had sounded for the House of Commons. Blue power suit, white silk blouse, heels. Impressive at this hour of the morning. Impressive and aggressive. With secret relief, Wiley got her a chair and left it all to Strauss, closing the door behind him.

Silence reigned.

Still the inspector did not turn around.

Finally, Isabella Roberts cleared her throat and crossed her legs.

"Well, Jerry," said the voice he would know forever, "aren't you at least going to say hello to your ex-wife?"

Chapter 6: Mutability

INGLESIDE 8:00 a.m.

Jerry turned to face the woman.

"My ex-wife?" he asked flatly.

Isabella had the grace to blush.

"We lived together for years, Jerry," she answered smoothly. "Got engaged. Just didn't make it to the altar."

"That wasn't my fault, Bella" he shot back, and then could have bitten his tongue for lapsing into the old nickname. "And this isn't about old times. It's about the dead woman upstairs. Did you know Audrey North?"

It hit him.

He was tired. He was old. He couldn't do this anymore. Audrey was dead and he didn't care. He wanted his bed and to get the hell away from this woman.

Something he'd read years ago flittered through his brain, about how the baby boomers couldn't handle aging. How the problem was they'd stayed young too long. Not him. Hell, he'd become old at twelve—the day his father died.

Strauss sat down, eyes on the desk.

She leaned back and crossed her legs. "You look tired, Jerry. You know, of course, I don't have to do this without my lawyer."

"Are you saying you need one?"

The two locked eyes for a moment, and then Bella laughed. "The gloves are off. I'm glad. I'd hate to be formal with you after all these years." She smiled warmly. "It *is* good to see you, you know."

Strauss absently picked up his pen and flipped it end over end on the desktop. Then he threw it down and folded his hands.

"Minister Roberts," he repeated quietly, "did you know Audrey North?"

Her smile vanished. "You're still angry with me, aren't you?"

"Have you had breakfast, Minister?" Jerry crossed his arms. "It might help to clear your head."

Isabella rose and turned for the door. "I don't do breakfast, Inspector. It slows me down. And I don't do interviews without my lawyer."

"Sit down, Bella." The tone was unmistakable. Roberts sat down. But this was Isabella, a woman who took no prisoners in her private life and had made a name for herself in the political arena for taking out her opponents with surgical precision. Jerry knew better than to be impressed with his own authority. She had her reasons. "How about coffee? I could use one myself."

She shook her head. "Let's just get this over with, Inspector. I have a very busy day today."

"And I have a dead woman upstairs. There might be some changes to your schedule."

Roberts opened her mouth and Jerry put up his hand.

"I know. I can't hold you here forever and, if I try, you'll have a dozen Mounties here on horseback to rescue you. Your banquet isn't until seven tonight," he continued, "and if I remember the agenda correctly, publicly you are set for a media conference this morning in one hour, followed by a lunch and some touring around . . . Would you reschedule for later this morning? Meet the media closer to noon?"

"And sit around here?"

"Might not be a bad idea, Bella. You want your press conference to focus on your announcements for the tourism in this area, not on the fact that you're in the middle of a homicide investigation. That wouldn't be good publicity, would it?" he asked pointedly.

She didn't reply.

"And I need a few quiet hours to do my job. I don't need a media scrum to deal with while I nail this thing down."

"Or the RCMP arriving to take over, right?"

It was Strauss's turn to not reply.

Finally, Isabella sighed. "Fine. We each need a favour. I'll head off the dogs at the pass until this lunch and you keep a lid on this with the press until tomorrow. What are you going to do about Bradshaw? He's inside."

"He's also 'assisting' me in my inquiries for the time being. I'll handle Bradshaw. Now . . . did you know Audrey North?"

Strauss noted a brief flicker in her eyes.

"No, not in the real sense of the word," said Roberts. "I had seen her a few times at different party functions over the past while. I don't know exactly what she did for a living, but she was after some political ties."

"Did you see her here yesterday? Talk to her?"

"No. I got here around three p.m. and went straight to my

room. Even ate supper there. Spent most of my time on the cell or the laptop."

"Did you hear anything unusual in the night?"

"No."

"Do you still use sleeping pills?"

Isabella cocked her head at him and smiled. "So you remember."

"Just answer the question."

"Sometimes."

"Why are you here, Bella?"

She looked at him. "For the conference and the banquet, of course. To promote what the federal government is going to do for the Seaway area."

"I mean, what are you doing *here*? At Sterling House?" Jerry got up and looked out the window. "It's a beautiful old home, but I would imagine you're used to five-star accommodations. And do you usually travel alone?"

She was silent so long that he turned to look at her.

"I'm not alone," she answered finally. "Matt Corning, my aide, should be here any minute to brief me for the day before the car arrives. But, yes, I usually stay at the large hotels. On the record, I wanted to stay here to enjoy first-hand some of the local tourist sites we are about to help promote."

"On the record? I'm not the media, Bella. I'm the police. No promises."

"Maybe. Maybe not." Isabella looked directly at him. "This has to do with you, Jerry. It's not police business. It's personal. I decided to stay here at Sterling House to have a chance to see you. Quietly. Without anyone getting the wind up."

"The wind up? About me?"

"Yes. About you. I'm in trouble, Jerry. Possibly big trouble. And you're the only one who can help me."

Strauss's cell phone rang. When he saw the number, he excused himself and went into the den, closing the door behind him.

Jerry flipped open the phone. "Superintendent Holland?"

"Strauss, just checking in," came the voice. "How is Minister Roberts? Everything going smoothly there?"

"Yes, sir." Strauss said crisply. Checking in, my ass, he thought. Checking up was more like it. Fine, Holland, he smiled grimly to himself. Two can play the game. "Minister Roberts is fine. We do have a situation here with . . ." Strauss put his hand over the cell phone, ". . . a possible homicide at the bed and breakfast . . ." and removed it again. "But everything is under control. We'll have her at the banquet with bells on."

"I didn't quite catch that, Strauss. You're breaking up."

"I said we'll have the minister at the banquet no problem."

"Did you say you had a situation there?"

"Sir? You seem to be breaking up."

"Call me on a land line, Strauss."

"Superintendent?" Jerry covered the mouthpiece again. "You're gone. I can't hear you." He moved his hand. "The phones here are out." Hand again. "Line's dead." Jerry moved his hand away once more, then held the cell out to arm's length. "If you can still hear me, sir, I'll check in with you as soon as I get back to the detachment."

He pushed the red phone icon to disconnect, a ghost of a smile on his face.

"In about six hours," he said to the den.

"There's someone at the front door." Mildred stood in the doorway, spatula in hand. "Do I answer it? And are you eating? I'd like to clean up the kitchen. And get dressed—if you don't mind."

Jerry moved past her into the dining room. It was empty, except for Stan North who hung over his coffee like an umbrella. Constable Taylor came through the swing door from the front hall.

"Taylor," said Strauss, "have we done a walk-through of all the rooms?"

"All except the . . ." Taylor shot a look at Stan, ". . . the Norths' room, sir. It's sealed, of course. Sergeant Wiley is finishing up now."

"Where is Bradshaw?"

"Upstairs in his room. As is Hugh Keeps still."

Strauss dropped his voice.

"What about the house line? Did you check that?"

Taylor shot another look at Stan and made a scissors motion behind one hand.

Strauss looked at her, then away, puzzled.

The doorbell rang.

"Well?" asked Mildred again.

"Sausages," said Strauss.

"Just sausages? And what about the door?"

"Sausages and coffee." He looked at Taylor in her uniform, then turned to Mildred. "You get the door. Get rid of anyone you know and not a word just yet. Anyone you don't know, leave them in the front porch and get me."

"No toast?"

"No."

Spatula held high, Mildred pushed through the swing door and disappeared.

Taylor chanced a glance at Strauss.

"Shouldn't you have a meal, sir? You haven't slept, and—"

"Exactly, Taylor. Any carbs and I'll go down like a ton of bricks. The sausages will keep me awake. If the protein doesn't, the heartburn will."

"Yes, sir. I only—"

She broke off at the sound of voices coming through the living room. They turned to see a man in a suit followed by Mildred Keeps, spatula raised high as though she were going to hit him. Strauss half hoped she would. If this were Corning, Bella's aide, it would be one less ego on his to-do list if Mildred took him out.

"Where is Minister Roberts?" the man demanded. "Why can't I see her?"

"Matt Corning, I presume?" Strauss extended his hand. "Inspector Strauss, SD&G OPP."

Corning ignored the hand. "Has something happened to Isabella?"

"No," Strauss lowered his hand. He already disliked the man. The suit was expensive, the cologne cloying, the tie too perfect. Good God, the nails looked manicured. "She's being interviewed right now, but I can let you see her in a few minutes."

"What's going on here?" The man looked at Constable Taylor's uniform with only a brief stop at her face. "Why all the police?"

"We'll have a chat shortly," Jerry stonewalled. "Have a seat in the living room till I come for you."

"Somebody killed my wife," said Stan North.

Corning opened his mouth and Strauss cut him off.

"Taylor, see that Mr. Corning is comfortable in the living room. I'll be right back."

Jerry strode back to the office, where Isabella waited by the window in the pool of morning sun. The light caught her blonde hair, making it glow. She was still beautiful, still flawlessly packaged. For just a moment, the years faded and uninvited memories rushed in.

A quiet, rainy afternoon in the sunroom, in the house they'd shared in Kingston. Jerry in a T-shirt and boxers. Bella in her long, white terry bathrobe, one shoulder exposed where the robe had slipped down, long blonde hair covering the other. Having just indulged in their favourite passion, Bella was into her second favourite—a cutthroat game of chess.

He moved a piece into her territory.

"Check, woman," he smiled.

She looked at the board, then smiled back. Slyly, she moved a piece toward him.

Jerry considered the move for a moment.

"But that will let me take out your queen, Bella. You do see that, don't you?"

Bella leaned across the board, the housecoat revealing now a lot more than a shoulder. She kissed him softly, then sat back.

"Any piece is expendable to save the king, Jerry. Never forget that."

Somehow, despite the intimacy, he couldn't shake the feeling she was talking about him, not to him.

And he'd been right. Bella had won the game that day, and later the game he hadn't known was their relationship. Not love, not trust, not partnership. Business. Business, pure and simple.

"Don't take it personally, Jerry," Bella had said when she left a few months later. "I can't marry you because of me. Not you. It just won't work for me. I have . . . things to do."

And she had walked out the door and never come back.

Just like his father. Just like Daniel. He remembered how, later that afternoon, he had quietly gone to the sunroom and packed up the chess set she'd left behind.

He'd put the king in last.

But Bella had returned after all these years. Why? And why here?

Strauss looked at her again, as though seeing her for the first time.

Blonde, but the wrong blonde. And the right blonde was not here.

"Farran Mackenzie, come home," he muttered.

Mildred swept in from behind, coffee and sausages in hand. She slammed them both down on the desk.

"Kitchen is closed," she said curtly, and left.

Jerry and Bella looked at the sausages and then each other.

"Matt Corning is here," said Jerry. "I'll bring him in here so you can talk. Will he keep quiet about this for now?"

"Matt won't say anything until I do."

Jerry went back to the living room and signalled Corning, who then almost beat him back to the office.

"Isabella—"

She waved him away. "Sit down, Matt. We have a problem and we need to rearrange my schedule. There's been an unexplained death here at the bed and breakfast, and the police need time today to start their investigation. Nobody is leaving just yet. "

Corning threw a dark look at Strauss, who sat behind the desk eating the sausages. "You're kidding, right? It took weeks to get everyone together for today."

"We're just rescheduling the media conference. Everything else is on as planned."

"But you're due there in an hour!" Corning ran his fingers through his hair. Somehow, it didn't move. "How can I change everybody's plans?"

Isabella sighed. "It will be a scramble." She looked at Jerry. "Is it really necessary for me to stay? *I* didn't kill the woman."

"Of course you didn't," Corning huffed. "If there is any insinuation on the part of the police . . . "

Strauss ignored the man. "Two hours," he said to Roberts. "Just a couple of hours, Bella."

She didn't answer for a minute, then turned to her aide. "You heard the man, Matt. That gives you an hour to make phone calls if you get started now. Let them know I will see them shortly before noon. Same location."

"What's this all about? I couldn't reach you on your cell phone."

Bella stood up. "I don't . . . Please just take care of it. Trust me, it's important. I'll explain later. And not a word about any problems here."

Corning looked murderously at Strauss, who continued to eat sausages.

There was a knock on the door and it opened to let Mildred steam in. She ignored Matt Corning who stepped back to let her through to Strauss. She grabbed the coffee mug and plate off the desk.

"I have to run my dishwasher now," she blurted, and made her escape.

"Who *is* that?" Corning turned to Strauss. "You should lock her up. She almost hit me with a spatula when I came in. The fashion police alone should arrest her for that housecoat."

"Okay, Mr. Corning," Jerry snapped into action, rising to take the man by the arm. "I have to see you to the door."

"I want an explanation," said Corning as Strauss steered him to the front door.

"We'll fill you in on a need-to-know basis." Strauss opened the front door and then the porch door. "Thank you for stopping by. Minister Roberts will be ready for you around ten-thirty."

Corning dug his heels in.

"This is a hell of a mess. Rescheduling will have a ripple effect today. That means I'll have to tell some people in very high places they have a change of plan. They aren't going to be very happy about that," he added ominously.

"I'm sure you can handle them," said Strauss smoothly. "I'm sure Bella works with only the best."

"Tread carefully, Inspector," Corning put his face in Jerry's. His skin was baby fine with not even a shaving shadow. Wasn't there something they do now with lasers? "You don't seem to see the big picture. We're coming in with several hundred thousand of promised programs and funding for this area. Whatever situation you have here has nothing to do with the minister—and better not catch her in the fallout. It could be your job at the end of the day."

Jerry's face went granite.

"It *is* my job, Corning. Not just at the end of the day, but twenty-four/seven. I am well aware of the minister's purpose for being here and what it means for the community. I am also aware that a human being has died violently and I may have a killer in this house. A killer it is my job to protect this same community from. And that's what I will do.

"As for the fallout," Jerry opened the porch door wider, "outside this house, it's your job. I suggest you get on it."

If one thing was clear to Jerry Strauss by the end of Mildred's interview, it was this: the woman was frightened.

Not uncomfortable, not uneasy, not nervous.

Frightened.

And not used to feeling out of control.

They sat in the office, Isabella having returned to her room, sweeping through the dining room without a glance at Bradshaw or at North, who now reclined on the living room davenport.

With the prim posture and the posh British accent, interviewing Mildred felt almost like grilling Mary Poppins in her retirement. Almost. Strauss glanced at her feet. The pink mules didn't fit the image.

"How long have you owned Sterling House?" asked Wiley. Since Wiley and Millie were now plant pals, Jerry let Wiley handle the questions. He sat off to her right, just enough in her peripheral vision to maintain his presence.

"Five years," said the woman, "in June. I was widowed. My uncle had a little money and wanted to get out of the nursing home, so we bought this together. He's lived with me ever since."

"He's quite elderly."

Millie hazarded a quick glance in Strauss's direction at his remark.

"Yes." She dropped her eyes to the floor. "Over ninety."

"It must be a bit of burden for you to run this business and care for an elderly man."

This time she did not raise her eyes.

"I was a nurse for twenty years. I'm trained to do it. He's actually my husband's uncle," she added, "but he's the only family I have left."

"You have a lovely older home," said Wiley. "Are you very busy with guests?"

"It pays the bills. I run afternoon teas as well."

"You have a full house right now?"

"Yes. All the rooms are taken."

"I'm surprised the minister didn't insist on having the place to herself," Jerry interjected.

Millie looked at his shoes.

"She couldn't. I was already booked. I couldn't even give her the Brass Room with the private sitting room, but she said she didn't care. Insisted on staying here regardless."

"Has Ms. Roberts been here before, Mrs. Keeps?"

Millie shook her head. "No. This is the first time."

"The Norths have been, though." Wiley looked at his notes.

"Yes. They've come for the past few years, usually in May.

Just once a year." The woman began to rock slowly in her seat. "And Mr. Bradshaw came here last month." She raised her chin but still not her eyes. "Did a piece on my bed and breakfast for *The Citizen* travel section."

"When did they all arrive?"

"Everybody came yesterday. In the afternoon. Before supper. Everyone had supper in their rooms," she sniffed. "Up and down with trays. Glad I don't usually do that. Be the death of me."

"You don't usually serve supper to your guests, Mrs. Keeps?" Jerry asked quietly.

"Of course not," she snapped. "It's called a bed and breakfast for a reason."

"Then why . . ."

Mildred kept her eyes trained on the floor. "Because the minister insisted on eating here for privacy. Arrived with her secretary, sent him packing and holed up in her room. That's where she ate supper. The others asked to do so as well, so I served them all. Charged for it accordingly," she added dryly.

"How did the Norths seem to you last night, Mrs. Keeps?" Wiley asked. "Were they in good spirits? Did they fight about anything?"

"No. He was cheerful as usual. She was . . . she was Audrey." Millie hesitated and then added, "Audrey North was not what you'd call a warm and fuzzy person. People skills weren't high on her list of priorities."

Coming from you that says a lot about Audrey North, Jerry thought. And nothing good.

"Did she seem upset or worried at all? Did she eat a good supper?"

Millie thought about Wiley's question for a moment, then shrugged. "I guess she ate well. Her plate was empty when I picked it up. And she seemed fine to me."

"Did your uncle eat in his room as well?"

Mildred finally looked at Strauss, the flicker of fear first showing in her eyes.

"Yes. He always does. Rarely leaves his room for long. Can't do the stairs well and that sort of thing. He's old," she added unnecessarily. "He couldn't have had anything to do Audrey's death."

The officers looked at each other.

"What time did you lock up for the night?" Wiley asked.

"Ten p.m. Then I set the alarm."

"And everyone was in at that time?"

"Yes, or I wouldn't lock up."

"In their rooms for the night?"

Again, a brief flicker in her eyes.

"Yes."

"Did you hear anything unusual in the night?"

"No." Mildred hesitated, then added, "No, nothing."

"Do you take anything to help you sleep, Mrs. Keeps?"

Both Wiley and Mildred looked at Strauss at his question.

"I do keep something handy. Why?"

"Tell us about this morning, Mrs. Keeps."

She faced front, crossed her arms and returned her gaze to the floor.

"I already told your constable, and I was just told I still haven't served all the breakfasts yet." The woman rose, but Wiley put up his hand.

"Please, Mrs. Keeps. It's been a trying morning for you, I'm sure, but we'd like to hear it from you, if you could." He gave her his best smile.

She relented but remained standing.

"I usually get up around five-thirty and start things in the kitchen. I was back in my own bathroom upstairs when Stan pounded on the door and yelled about calling 911. Said Audrey was dead. I tried to hush him up, of course. Thought he was drinking or something and didn't want the others getting all riled up. I went in his room and there she was with the knife sticking out of her. So I came out, locked the door and went out to your constable in the car to tell her what happened. Can I go now?"

Wiley looked at Strauss, who nodded.

Mildred beat it to the door, but Strauss's voice caught her before she could make a successful getaway.

"Mrs. Keeps, is there anyone in this house who would have reason to want Audrey North dead?"

She stood for a moment with her back to them, hand on the office doorknob. When she turned, her face was white.

"I really have no idea," Millie said, and then vanished.

"Coffee," said Strauss. "Maybe she could bring the machine in here." He rubbed his eyes again and sat down heavily. "Comments, Wiley?"

Jordan was silent for a minute.

"Scared," he said finally. "Protective of her uncle and feels there's a need to be in this situation, but more than in the usual way. She definitely knows something she isn't telling us, and from her reactions, I would say it's connected to the dead woman."

"I agree. I sense no love lost there, which is strange if the Norths have been only guests to Mildred. Maybe there's more. We need to get on the background checks. We've got a lot of blanks to fill in here." Jerry paused. "Mildred's definitely a scared woman, but it isn't for herself. Why would she be afraid for her uncle?"

Wiley reached out to the brogmansia, then thought better of it.

Strauss rose and stretched.

"Why don't we ask Hugh Keeps that question? I'll go up to speak to him. You start the background checks and babysit on this floor." He opened the office door. "No one talks to anyone else until we've talked to them."

"And I want to talk to you."

A tall man stood in the doorway. Constable Taylor brought up the rear, her face flushed with irritation.

"I'm sorry, Inspector. He barged through and wouldn't listen to me."

The man grinned. "Don't blame your charming officer, Strauss. You know what I'm like. Never was good at taking orders. And I have to go. Deadlines, you know." He stuck out a business card. "You can reach me here. And I'll need my cell phone back, sweetie," he added to Taylor.

Jerry gave him a dark look that any officer in SD&G knew enough to avoid.

"She's Constable Taylor to you, Bradshaw. And you're not going anywhere. At least not for a while."

The grin vanished. "Ah, come on, Strauss. I've got things to do."

"Let me say this in language you would understand," said Strauss dryly. "This is a homicide investigation. I have a woman upstairs dead and a lot of questions to answer before people start leaving. You are grounded for the next two hours."

Bradshaw turned grim.

"You can't do this. I know my rights in these situations."

"From much past experience, I'm sure." Jerry smiled. "I can hold you for questioning for twenty-four hours," he said pleasantly. "And if you give Constable Taylor any further trouble, she will detain you with any methods she sees fit."

At that, Buck grinned. "Now that sounds like fun." He looked at Taylor, who ignored him to look at Strauss.

"Sir?"

"Taylor," Strauss kept a straight face, "If you have to hurt him, make it permanent, will you?" He turned back to Bradshaw and beamed. "As I said, my charming constable can take you down to the interrogation room at the detachment or you can wait here, in the comfort of the Sterling House Bed and Breakfast. What will it be, Buck?"

The man fumed in silence for a moment, then ran his fingers through his hair, making the grey curls even wilder.

"Fine. You win this round, Strauss. But let's get my interview over with so I can have some breakfast. I'm starving."

"Fair enough." Jerry turned to give orders. "Wiley, check on North and Mildred Keeps. Warn her that the kitchen is open again. Have some food yourself if you haven't eaten and get that information we need. Taylor, have Keeps make a breakfast tray for the minister and take it up to her. Tell her that I'll be with her shortly. And send a tray in here for Mr. Bradshaw. This could take a while."

"The woman can cook." Buck Bradshaw finished off the last of the sausages and wiped his plate with his toast. "Have you ever tried her afternoon teas? Victorian teas. Everything homemade. I positively rolled out of here last month. But," he added with a grin, "man to man, watch out for the silver pie-lifter thingie. Got my finger stuck in the handle. Wasn't very cool."

"What brought you here last month, Bradshaw?" Jerry stood looking out the window, watching the quiet neighbourhood come to life for the day. Kids waiting for the school bus. A woman walking to the mall. Two dogs out for their morning constitutional. A normal, pleasant scene. Yet not the one that belonged out of these windows . . .

Buck pushed the empty plate away and picked up his coffee.

"Been hearing that the old place was a bed and breakfast," he replied, crossing his legs. "Was curious about how it looked now. Pitched the article to the *Citizen* with the Seaway history and the ghost legend. They took it so here I was."

Jerry sat down at the desk and looked across at Buck. The man still had the habit of talking with his mouth while listening with his eyes. Constantly thinking. Constantly maintaining surveillance. He'd been like that as a boy, too.

"So why are you here now?"

The man dropped his eyes, then shrugged. "Covering the minister's visit."

"The *Citizen* would have their own people on that, not a freelance," Jerry said simply.

Buck shrugged again. "Never hurts to be where the action is. Never know what you might end up with." He set his cup down and leaned forward with a grin. "Isn't it something, Jerry? The two of us back in this house again. And Audrey, too, even though she can't join us. Who knows, maybe Daniel Sterling's ghost will show up. Voices from the Lost Villages and all that."

SUPERSONIC ATOMIC BOMBER
UNVEILED BY U.S. AIR FORCE

QUEEN TO OPEN HOUSE

OTTAWA (CP)—For the first time in history, a reigning monarch is to open Canada's parliament. Prime Minister Diefenbaker's office announced Tuesday that the first session of Canada's new parliament will be opened by the Queen on Monday, Oct. 14, during a five-day visit to Canada.

Water Supply, Sewers Big Rehabilitation Job

One of the major problems facing the St. Lawrence Seaway Authority in its transportation of people and towns in the Seaway Valley is the provision for adequate water facilities. The creation of a man-made lake extending some 30 miles upstream in the St. Lawrence River will mean the flooding of 20,000 acres of land including seven villages along the shore. To accommodate the people, who have been required to move, additions have been made to both Iroquois and Morrisburg and two new towns, Long Sault and Ingleside, have been built.

Wednesday, July 10, 1957
The Cornwall *Standard Freeholder*

It was just the two of them at the swimming hole. A hot July day, and a silence sat over the water as it did over the last of the village. The girls' change hut was gone, as was the boathouse that the boys had used.

"Hey, kid!"

Jerry had been swimming quietly in his trunks, having been urged by Daniel to head for the water. His heart sank at the sound of the voice.

"Hi, Bucky," the boy replied reluctantly, turning to where the voice had come from only to get a face full of water from Buck's cannonball into the depths. The other boy came up blowing water and grinned.

"Isn't it something, Jerry? We got the whole thing to ourselves. Everybody must be too busy to drive out from the new town today."

"How come you're here?" Jerry asked.

Bucky shrugged.

"My mom dropped me off. She's down the road doin' a couple of errands."

"Errands?" Jerry thought a moment. "But there's no place left to do errands anymore."

Bucky just shrugged a second time.

"The mall in the new town ain't finished. Some things are still here."

He dove back under the water.

Half an hour later, they walked back along the road toward the Sterling house. As they came abreast of the Beckett farm, shouting could be heard from inside the house.

Bucky stopped in the road, listening.

Jerry was still walking when the front door of the Beckett house burst open and Beryl Bradshaw stormed out onto the porch.

"I'm sure your husband would like to know, Audrey Beckett!" she spat over her shoulder to the woman on her heels.

"There's nothing to tell him, Beryl Bradshaw," Audrey replied, "and if you say anything, you're responsible for what happens."

"Whatever happens, I hope it happens to you—and that good-for-nothing husband of mine . . ." She saw her son standing in the road and stopped on the steps. "Bucky—"

Buck whirled around and took off, back toward the swimming hole.

Jerry watched Beryl get in the truck to follow her son. Feeling eyes on himself, he turned and saw Audrey watching him closely.

Then she wordlessly went back into the house.

The screen door slammed and Jerry was alone.

Buck had retreated grudgingly to his room and Jerry was alone. He remembered those eyes, encased in a beautiful face with a soft voice, yet so cold. Cold as they had been staring at him from the face of death.

Maybe it hadn't been her fault. Maybe losing the Daniel she knew had broken her heart, and she'd married Joe Beckett to start a new life only to find heartbreak there, too.

But she had watched him. He didn't know why but he had felt her eyes on him every day.

"How are things going with your son, Mrs. Strauss?"

They were outside at the car, Jerry seeing his mother off after one of her visits. Daniel watched from the porch window.

At the question, Jerry and his mother turned to see Audrey Beckett walking toward them from her house.

"It is going very well, Mrs. Beckett," said Emme with a cool smile. "Thank you for asking."

"So, no problems with him?" Audrey turned to look at the Sterling house, and the porch curtains fell together.

"No," replied Emme crisply. "Why should there be? Jerry is being treated very well. Daniel says he is like the son he never had."

"Really?" Audrey smiled at the boy.

But somehow, the smile didn't reach her eyes.

"I need to talk to the inspector." Isabella glanced furtively at Bradshaw's closed door before turning back to smile stiffly at Constable Taylor sitting on a chair in the upstairs hallway.

"He's going over the crime scene right now, Minister Roberts, but I will let him know as soon as they're finished."

A murmur of voices could be heard from behind the closed door of the Brass Room.

Roberts looked at her watch grimly and then vanished.

"I'm getting hungry. What time is it?"

"I can't help you with that," said the girl. The darkness in the tiny room seemed lighter somehow, as though sunlight was seeping through the walls. There was a small crack of light coming from under the old door, and voices could be heard from a nearby room.

"It's still too soon, too dangerous for you to leave," she continued. "Sleep. You've been up all night. Sleep for a while."

Jerry wanted sleep. The bed in the Brass Room, even with its grim occupant, looked inviting. Just a few minutes . . .

"I checked the wall on the other side of the sitting room that connects to the other sitting room," said Wiley.

Strauss had released Bradshaw to the safety of his room and joined the sergeant there for another look. They were both standing just inside the door to the bedroom itself, not making any inroads to the little sitting room facing the door. Strictly confined access in this room until ident arrived or the officers would have a hairy bear fit on him.

"And?" Jerry yawned.

"And the wall has been filled in, the wallpaper intact. Unless there is something like a secret door in the sitting room, I don't see any other way in here except this door." Wiley indicated the door to the hall.

Jerry nodded grimly, then gingerly lifted the sheet over the corpse. He looked carefully at the knife. Something about it . . .

"What is it, sir?" Wiley snuck a peek with him.

"The knife, sergeant." Strauss carefully laid the sheet back down. "There's something about it that seems familiar, but I can't place it. For some reason, I think the blade is shorter than the handle. Still," he added, "it was no mean feat to stab Audrey in the chest right up to the hilt of the knife. It was quite the attack."

"It would take a certain amount of strength," Wiley agreed.

"Strength, Wiley, or . . . " Strauss considered the corpse's form under the sheet, " . . . or hatred."

They had started on the garage. Daniel had given Jerry breaks but none for himself, working relentlessly in the cruel sun. Jerry watched him all day—attacking the building, more beating it down than tearing it down.

At one point, Daniel stopped and stood a long time, just staring at the wreckage on the ground. Jerry watched him silently, then carefully went to him and put one hand on his arm.

The misshapen face was filled with tears.

"It's all shit, son," he whispered. "All shit." One hand he placed gently on Jerry's head. The other tossed the axe on the pile of boards.

Without another word, Daniel headed back into the house. Jerry saw Audrey watching him from her back porch and followed the man inside.

Supper was silent.

When he went to his room for bed, Jerry opened the door and walked into a sweet, flowery scent. Startled, he looked around for some flowers sitting somewhere—and then it hit him.

Violets?

His heart thumping, the boy moved into the room and looked into the closet. Nothing. Under the bed. Nothing. The smell was gone and he wasn't sure he hadn't imagined it.

Then he brushed his hair in the mirror—and saw her standing behind him. Whirling around, the boy dropped the brush and stood back against the dresser.

The room was empty.

"Daniel? Daniel!" Jerry ran down the hall and pounded on Daniel's door. He burst into the room, found the bed empty and saw the light on in the sitting room.

"Daniel, I saw her. I saw Harriet."

Daniel was sitting in the chair just around the corner, a book open in his lap and a bottle beside him. He held a pencil in his hand that he flipped over and over on end.

"You saw her?" A slow smile cracked the twisted features. "Pullin' my leg, aren't you, son?"

"No, no," Jerry replied breathlessly. "In the mirror. I saw her in the mirror. And I smelt the flowers."

Daniel looked troubled, but did not speak.

Jerry looked around the room. Here it was clean and tidy, the shelves filled with more books and no pictures. He turned to the book in Daniel's lap.

"Watcha readin'?"

Daniel picked up the book.

"Percy Bysshe Shelley," he said. "Poetry. One of the great Romantic poets."

Jerry wrinkled his nose.

"That's girl stuff."

"Hardly." Daniel slapped the book shut. "'For, be it joy or sorrow,'" he quoted from memory, "'The path of its departure is still free: Man's yesterday may ne'er be like his morrow; Nought may endure but Mutability.'"

"What's mutability?"

"Change," Daniel replied, a dark look crossing his face. "That's what life is all about. Change." He took a swig from the bottle. "Change and shit. But the man believed that we must cling to hope. It is our moral obligation." He considered the glass for a minute, then set it down. "Get on to bed now."

Jerry hesitated, thinking of Harriet.

"Um, could I have something to read?" he asked.

Daniel looked at him a moment, then rose and selected several volumes from his shelves. Milton's Paradise Lost, Frankel's Man's Search For Meaning, Mary Shelley's Frankenstein, and the collected works of Matthew Arnold. On top of that, he put the book of Shelley he'd been reading and handed the pile to Jerry.

"That should keep you for a bit," he said.

When Jerry sat in bed and opened the book of Shelley, a paper and a picture fell out from where Daniel had used them as bookmarks. The photograph showed a happy couple, a younger Audrey and a handsome man Jerry did not recognize. Then he realized it was Daniel, as he had looked before the accident. Jerry looked at the picture for a long time before opening the paper. It was a handwritten will done by Daniel in 1944, in case he did not return from duty, leaving everything to his fiancée, Audrey Connelly.

Realizing he was reading something private, Jerry folded the paper up and put it with the photograph. He headed out to Daniel's room and tapped carefully on the door. When there was no response, the boy slowly opened the door. The bed was again empty and two shoes were seen peeking around the corner of the sitting room.

Jerry found Daniel asleep in the chair, a copy of Dante's Inferno now beside him on the table, along with the bottle and glass. The boy wondered for just a minute how a man who never left his home got liquor in a dry township. Then he carefully slid the paper and photograph into the book and left the room.

On the table next to the bed, there was an old copy of Dante's Inferno sitting on the table. Jerry carefully picked up the book and flipped open the cover. Inside was a startlingly familiar scrawl.

Daniel Sterling.

Strauss slapped the book shut.

"Mrs. Keeps, it's time I spoke with your uncle."

Jerry stood in the kitchen, helping himself to another coffee. Mildred had brewed it strong, and even the smell seemed to lift the fog a little.

Mildred's head snapped up from the papers, bank statements and cancelled cheques strewn across the kitchen table in the breakfast nook. It was the only sign of chaos in the immaculate kitchen.

"He has nothing to do with this, Inspector. He's over ninety, very frail and easily upset."

"I understand," Jerry stood over the table. "But I have to speak with everyone. He may have seen or heard something and not realize its importance."

"I don't see how." The woman rubbed her hands together as though she were cold. "He's half blind and half deaf. This won't do anything except upset him, possibly land him in hospital again."

"You can be there. We'll have a quiet chat in his room. It won't take long."

Mildred dropped her eyes, hesitated, then slowly rose from the table.

"Jerry, I—" Isabella burst into the room and then stopped. She looked at Mildred for a moment, then continued. "Inspector, I still need a word with you."

"Shortly, Ms. Roberts," said Jerry. "I have to speak with someone right now."

"It can't wait."

He looked at her, surprised at the fluster. It was not the Isabella he remembered, nor the face he'd watched on TV over the intervening years.

"Very well. Let's use the office. Mrs. Keeps, I'll be right back."

"Does this have something to do with Audrey North's death?" Jerry curled his hand around the coffee mug on the desk.

Isabella looked out the window.

"No. It's personal."

"And it has to do with me."

"Yes."

"We were over a long time ago," said Jerry flatly. "This must be about ancient history."

"History is never ancient," she replied cryptically. "It keeps coming back, whether we like it or not."

Farran's face flashed into his mind. When would she be home?

"You sound like a friend of mine, Bella. Shoot. I've no time to waste today."

She opened her mouth, closed it again, then spoke.

"I told you earlier that I'm in trouble. Possibly big trouble." Isabella sighed. "It has to do with an episode in my life shortly after I left you. A relationship I pursued. I've kept it hidden all these years because of the implications, but someone knows. Or thinks they know."

"A past relationship that can hurt you now?" Jerry looked skeptical. "Christ, Bella, it's the twenty-first century. Even an illegitimate child in your past wouldn't leave a dent. You'd have to have ties to Adolf Hitler."

"I'm talking about Michael Andrew Browning."

Strauss sat back. Michael Andrew Browning. Late media king, power puppeteer, notorious alleged bosom buddy with more than one Mafia kingpin. The implications would be enormous for anyone in Parliament.

"You were involved with Browning?"

"Yes." She looked at the floor. "We were lovers. For almost a year. When I found out how bad it was with him, I left. He was killed some months later."

"And then your career in politics took off."

"Right."

Something she said . . .

"You left me in the spring, Bella." Jerry looked at her hard. "Browning died in the fall of that same year, I seem to remember. But you just said you were lovers for almost a year."

She kept her eyes on the floor.

He did the math.

"And now," he said finally, "you're here to ask for a favour. Must be a whopper after *that* bombshell."

Dead silence.

Jerry got up and started for the door.

"Leaving you for him was the greatest mistake of my life." Isabella's words stopped him at the door. "I make no excuse about that. But this isn't about me—or even you. It's about someone else." When Strauss didn't move, she continued. "The relationship was brief. I covered my tracks afterward pretty well. All except one thing that couldn't be hidden. And someone has dug it up. If they prove it, if they prove the connection, it will all come to light and look bad. Very bad. My entire career could come under fire and everything I've worked for put on ice. Even this big package I've swung for the Seaway Valley. The press will look for payoffs in every direction. The fallout could come this far."

"How can *I* possibly help you, Bella—if for any reason I should?"

She took a deep breath and let it go.

"This isn't easy to say. It all sounds so self-serving, so mercenary. But it's not. It was human error and bad judgment." Isabella was silent for a moment. "Shortly after Michael died, I gave birth to a baby. A boy. A beautiful child. I gave him up for adoption. I put your name on the birth certificate as the father. If you deny the claim, there will be enough room for doubt that Mike was the father of that baby. If this story goes public, I need you to stand by that claim."

"The timing . . ."

"The timing will work. Just."

Strauss jammed his fists in his pockets. At that moment, he needed a lot more than caffeine. He needed a stiff shot, and it made him think fondly of Farran and her penchant for brandy. Brandy would be just the ticket, right now. Brandy. And Farran Mackenzie.

"So," he turned to her, "what you are saying is you need me to lie for you?"

Isabella slowly rose to face him, seeming to draw in all her strength to do it.

"No, I'm asking you to not fight the claim. That's all."

"But that's lying."

"No, Jerry," she said slowly. "That's just it. It wouldn't be lying. It would be the truth."

She took a deep breath and let it out.

"Jerry, you *were* the father of that baby."

Chapter 7: Wales 1957

Just as Dickinson's Landing replaced the Hoople Settlement when the stagecoach appeared, the village of Wales one mile inland replaced the Landing as the centre of commerce and activity with the completion of the Grand Trunk Railway. Hoople's Creek ran through the west end of the Village and at Inundation time the flood waters uprooted nearly 200 people many of whom were descendants of the United Empire Loyalists . . . Following the completion of the Grand Trunk Railway in the 1850's the hamlet became known as Dickinson's Landing Station serving Dickinson's Landing one mile south. In 1860 Edward, Prince of Wales, later Edward VII, came up by train from Montreal to shoot the Longue Sault Rapids at Dickinson's Landing. He is said to have asked why the little place did not have a name of its own. Shortly after, the people made application for a post office and requested the village be named Wales after the prince.
—Rosemary Rutley, *Voices from the Lost Villages*

FIRST AIR-TO-AIR ATOMIC ROCKET FIRED
15,000 Feet In Air; Desert Sun "Paled"
Scorpion Jet Launches A-Headed "Genie"
Rocket From Formation Of Three Planes

New CNR Line In Operation This Sunday

C.N.R. officials reported yesterday that all trains will operate over the 40-mile diversion route between Iroquois and Cornwall on July 21. No special ceremony is planned to mark the full-scale opening of the route, which is the longest piece of main-line double track laid in Canada in many years. Starting July 22 at 1:35 a.m., the trains will all run on the new line. The first passenger train to run over the new line will be No. 17 from Montreal—the "overnight sleeper" to Toronto that passes through Cornwall at 12:37, Standard Time. Five new stations will open for passenger, freight express and telegraph business at Cornwall, Long Sault, Ingleside, Morrisburg and Iroquois. The present stations along the old line connecting Iroquois, Morrisburg, Aultsville, Farran's Point, Moulinette, Milles Roches and Cornwall will be closed.

Friday, July 19, and Saturday, July 20, 1957
The Cornwall *Standard Freeholder*

The Village of Wales was the only inland village about to be lost to the flooding. Hoople's Creek, the pretty little waterway that meandered through the village and surrounding farms, had been the crux of life for everyone for several generations, especially the children who swam, skated and played on its banks year-round. Now, as the access for the floodwaters set to rise within the year, the creek would bring the shore of the new headpond one mile inland to create Hoople's Bay, washing out the farmlands and the village forever. Ironically, what had sustained colonial life in that area for over 200 years had now signed its death warrant.

For the last time after a century of service, the Moccasin had pulled into the Wales station promptly at twenty minutes to eight that morning. The old train, nicknamed long ago for the Mohawk who once travelled on her, had been the lifeline through the villages, delivering mail and cargo between Brockville and Montreal on the Grand Trunk for over a century. As it had been now for a year, the station platform was almost deserted. There were few villagers left to bring their mail or catch a ride to Cornwall for the day, no hatchery to deliver chicks and eggs bound for Montreal, no children to watch the unloading from the train of any cargo from Brockville. The barbershop had closed and moved to New Town No. 1, now called Ingleside, so no one there having an early shave or gossip to watch the train from the window.

No one but a young man named Jerry Strauss.

"Hmph," Daniel had said that morning from behind the Standard Freeholder at breakfast. "No word on that Monroe murder in Maple Grove yet. I say it's the wife. It's always the wife. And," he added ominously, "train's last run today. End of an era, and not a good thing. Just another thing ground under the wheels of change, son."

"The new track north of here will take over tomorrow," Jerry had pointed out, shovelling ham and eggs into his mouth. "The trains will keep going."

"Not the same," had come the ominous reply. "The Grand Trunk built this village out of a hamlet in the forest and a few farms, just like the stage coach built the Landing south of here. The new stations are outside the new villages, I hear. If you can't walk then it's not a part of village life. No one will care when the trains roll in. And when they get that new highway, the 401, built, that will take most of the traffic away."

"I'm goin' to watch the Moccasin come in, then." Jerry had drunk his milk in a gulp, then wiped his mouth on his sleeve. "Comin' with me, Daniel?"

The eyes over the paper had given him his answer. No.

The silence at the station was eerie. Even after three years of watching houses being moved and villages emptying into the new towns, Jerry couldn't get used to the silence where so much life used to be. Most of Wales was gone, now just a cross-stitch of empty roads, tree stumps and filled-in foundations. With nothing to break the view, Jerry could look north to see the hulking presence of the Sterling house, standing almost alone now where the village used to be. Across the street, the barber's house and shop were boarded up, slated for coming demolition.

And after today, not even the steam whistle of the Moccasin would break the silence here.

"Passenger?" The conductor smiled at the boy.

"No, sir. Just watchin'. They open the new track tomorrow?"

"It's been open since May," the man replied. "Been sendin' the slow freights over it to tamp it down. The first passenger run comes through from Montreal to Toronto tonight. The No. 17 overnighter. It'll pass through around here just after midnight."

There was nothing more to say. The boy waited on the platform, watching the few passengers from Brockville look at the decimated village from their seats. Despite the lack of traffic at the station, the train waited the customary twenty minutes before building steam to leave.

At promptly 8:00 a.m., July 21, 1957, the Moccasin steam train left the Wales station bound for Montreal, for the last time.

The voices from the Sterling house carried in the silent village.

"I'm no part of it and you know it, Joe. Now leave my house and leave me alone."

"There's no one else. And she's always felt sorry for you . . . "

There was the sound of something hitting the floor. Jerry ran up the steps and through to the living room to see Daniel holding Joe by the collar, a dining room chair lying on its back..

"I don't need or want pity, especially from your wife," Daniel said flatly. "She couldn't look at me ten years ago. Why should she now?" He released Joe slowly. "I just want to be left alone. Leave me be. I'm sorry for your troubles but—"

"I don't need your pity, either," Joe growled. "We both know who the coward is." He turned and stalked out of the house, ignoring the boy standing silently near the door.

Daniel watched him leave, then walked into the dining room. Uncorking the decanter, he poured a shot in a small glass and threw it back. He turned and saw Jerry, who had followed him into the room. Daniel held up the glass as if in a toast.

"See, son?" he shook his head. "More shit."

"You, lad. Jerry Strauss."

At the voice, the boy looked up from the garden where he was hoeing. Mrs. Bradshaw stood nervously across the yard at the fence between the Sterling and Beckett properties. She looked over her shoulder and then back at Jerry, motioning him to come over.

Jerry put down the hoe and obeyed. When he reached the woman, she leaned down to whisper.

"Have you seen my son today?"

"Buck?" Jerry shook his head. "No, ma'am. Not today. Why?"

"He wasn't home this morning when I got up." She pulled at her hem. "I . . . I thought he might come here." She looked over at the Beckett house again.

"Did you check at the barn?" Jerry suggested. "I seen Mr. Bradshaw out there quite a bit lately. I guess he's runnin' out of time like we are."

The woman flushed, her lips making a thin line. "Yes," she said grimly. "Yes, you are right, Jerry Strauss. Rowdy Bradshaw has run out of time."

Jerry put the hoe back in the workshed, and closed the door. Out of habit, he looked up at the Beckett house and thought he saw a figure at an upstairs window. Then it was gone.

He went back to the garden and got down on his knees to weed. Over his shoulder, he heard the back screen door bang and the sound of furtive footsteps on the path.

"Hey, son," Daniel hissed, head low. "Your mother's on the telephone for you."

Jerry rose on his knees in time to see Audrey Beckett steal through the fence gate and up behind Daniel.

"Daniel?"

The man whirled around to face her, then started toward the house.

"Daniel!" She grabbed him by the arm. "You have to help me. You have to talk to Joe." Her voice rose shrilly. "Just look at me."

From where he knelt, Jerry could see her face. One eye was swollen and bruised.

Daniel stopped in his tracks. "Audrey," he said softly.

The woman reached out with her other hand to gently touch his face. They stood together for a moment, then Daniel abruptly pulled free and strode to the house. Jerry ducked behind the corn and waited. Audrey remained for a few minutes, looking at the house. Then she was gone.

It was the hottest part of the day. Jerry walked over to Hoople's Creek for a quick swim before supper, and found Buck there alone, skipping stones from a rock.

He braced himself for the usual antagonism. Curiously, there was none. The other boy looked over at Jerry and then went on skipping stones into the creek, saying nothing.

"Hey, Bucky," Jerry ventured.

"Hey." The boy did not look up.

"Your ma is lookin' for you, ya know. She came to the house to ask me if I'd seen you."

At that, the boy's head snapped up.

"She was at the Beckett house?" he said accusingly. "Was my pa there, too?"

Jerry shrugged and waded into the creek. "I didn't see him if he was." He dove in. The water was delicious. He came up spluttering, shaking his bangs out of his eyes. "You goin' to see the train off tonight?" he asked.

But he was alone. Buck had gone.

Supper was eaten in silence. Daniel had barely spoken since the encounter with Audrey that afternoon. He seemed preoccupied and Jerry did not ask him about it.

Some of the china was sitting out in boxes beside them, the boxes partly packed. Just the sideboard had been emptied, and a few pictures taken down on the wall above it.

And Mary Hoople's knife was gone.

Daniel sat in the front porch with the windows open for the evening breeze, a small bottle beside him on the table.

"I'm goin' to see the train tonight," said Jerry. He waited. "Come with me," he added finally.

Daniel shook his head. "You know I can't do that, son. Can't have people looking' at me."

"But there was no one at the station this morning," Jerry protested. "It's the last run ever here, Daniel. You can't miss it."

Daniel sighed and smiled sadly at the boy.

"Just another ending, Jerry. I've seen enough of those to last me now. I'll pass on this one."

Halfway to the station, Jerry heard a truck approaching and moved over to the side of the road. Turning, he watched Rowdy Bradshaw drive slowly past in his truck, alone. The man headed south toward Dickinson's Landing and his barn, but after crossing the CNR tracks, he turned into the abandoned hatchery. Jerry headed west to the train station.

At 8:20 p.m. sharp, the steam whistle of the Moccasin announced its arrival in Wales.

As though the past three years had not happened, the station was full of people. In unspoken agreement, many had returned from the new town to see the Moccasin come through Wales for the last time. The crowd was mostly silent, quiet murmurs here and there. It seemed unreal, even in the face of so much change, that the old train would not do this for another century on this track, let alone another day.

The old conductor got out, looked at the crowd and headed into the station. Five minutes, ten, fifteen. At twenty, he returned to the platform and faced the crowd.

"Passengers?" he asked sadly. When no one came forward, he nodded. For a moment, tears seemed to threaten. He pursed his lips and stepped up into the car.

"All aboard!" he yelled. The bells clanged, the engine hissed into life, the people moved back. The Moccasin began to move west out of the station, on its way to the next stop of Farran's Point. As if in salute to the remains of the village, the conductor hung out of the doorway, hand raised high. The people on the platform waved back and watched the old train move into the gathering sunset.

In the front of the crowd, Jerry Strauss stood gazing at the train as it went. The whistle shrieked once, twice, three times. At 8:40 p.m., July 21, 1957, the Moccasin headed west out of Wales and—as far as the village was concerned—into history.

"Daniel?"

The house was dark in the approaching dusk. The front porch was empty, as was the bottle beside the chair where Daniel had been sitting. Jerry went into the living room, only to find it empty and dark also. Dining room. Kitchen. He went out on the back porch and looked over at the barn and workshop. No lights. No lights or sign of life at the Beckett house either.

The boy went back into the house and up to his room. Looking around the corner, he saw that Daniel's bedroom door was closed.

"Daniel?" Jerry knocked hesitantly, then quietly opened the door. No Daniel asleep on the bed. The room was empty and dark.

But there was enough twilight coming in the windows of the little room beyond to show Jerry a pair of men's feet just inside the door. Someone was sitting in the reading chair.

"Daniel?" Jerry made his way around the bed without turning on a light. "I watched the train go through. You should have seen . . ."

The boy rounded the corner and stopped in the middle of the little room.

It was not Daniel Sterling in the reading chair. It was Joseph Beckett—or at least had been. The man was dead, a hole in his chest bleeding all over the bottom of his shirt and into his lap. His head was slumped back, eyes and mouth open as if in surprise at the sudden end of his life. His hunting rifle lay on the floor beside him.

Jerry stood for a moment, his own mouth open, eyes not registering the violence in front of him.

"Mother of God," he whispered.

A hand on his shoulder made him jump. Turning, he saw Daniel standing behind him where he had silently come out of the shadows. The man looked at the body of Joe Beckett grimly, then at the boy. The hand tightened.

"God's got nothing to do with this, son," he said quietly.

Chapter 8: Windows

Daniel's room. The Brass Room.

"I have to see the crime scene again." Jerry headed for the stairs with Wiley right behind.

"Sir? We still need ident to go over that room."

"I know. It's just that when we first arrived, I thought the knife in Audrey's chest looked familiar. Now I think I've placed it. I want to see if I'm right."

They stopped at the door to the Brass Room and Wiley unlocked it with the key. Jerry moved into the room carefully and lifted the sheet over the body on the bed. He looked at the knife.

"Just as I thought," he said grimly. "This knife came from this house. It belonged to Daniel Sterling and used to be displayed downstairs on the wall of the dining room. I haven't seen this in almost fifty years."

"So, if it comes from here, anyone could have used it last night," said Wiley.

"No, that's just it. If this is the same knife—and I believe it is—it was used to commit a murder in this room in 1957, but was never found after the fact."

Wiley looked at him.

"Precisely." Strauss closed the door with one finger and turned to Wiley in the room. "That means that this murder is connected to the murder of Joe Beckett. Or someone wants it to look that way. But where the hell did the knife come from after all these years?"

"Could Mildred Keeps have had it here, maybe found it when fixing up the place and didn't know what it was? Maybe it was out on display here, too."

"Let's ask her."

The door to Isabella's room was closed when Strauss passed by. He peeked into the living room on his way to the kitchen and saw Stan North snoring on the couch. In the dining room, Buck Bradshaw was making notes in a steno pad while trying to engage a reticent Constable Taylor in conversation. Mildred was filling the dishwasher when he pushed through the swing door to the kitchen.

"We need you upstairs, Mrs. Keeps."

"Do we have to interview my uncle?" she stiffened. "He's going to get all worked up."

"Yes, we do. So let's get it over with. But first I need you to identify something."

Millie grimaced and followed Strauss upstairs. He stopped at the door to the Brass Room.

"I need you to take a look at the murder weapon. I hope this won't be too much for you."

Millie sniffed. "I'm a retired nurse, for heaven's sake," she said. "I've seen it all at least once."

Strauss knocked on the door. When Wiley let them in, he moved to the bed and pulled back the sheet. "The knife, Mrs. Keeps," he said quietly. "Does it belong to you?"

He had to give her credit. Nerves of steel. She leaned in close over Audrey's still form to look at the handle protruding from the chest.

"Nope." She straightened up. "Never seen it before."

"You're sure?"

She gave Strauss a look. "Of course I'm sure. I know my things. Besides, the handle is quite distinctive, isn't it?"

"Yes, it is," Strauss agreed. So why use something so unique? he asked silently. Something is very weird here.

Weird. Okay, stick to protocol.

"Mrs. Keeps," he said firmly, "it's time to talk to your uncle. See if he can tell us anything."

Strauss headed out of the door, then stopped. He thought he saw a flash of white lace disappear around the corner of the hall in the direction of the stairs. With three strides, he made it to the corner, then the top of the stairs. Hall and stairs were empty and no sound of footsteps.

Violets. No mistaking it. All around him.

That's the flower she loved, son. Legend says that scent follows her spirit in the house. Never ran into it myself . . .

It was gone.

His eyes were burning and he shut them. "This is nuts, Strauss," he whispered. "This is not 1957. This is not Wales. There are no such things as ghosts." He looked around on the floor and on the hall table for anything to explain the scent. "Something very human is going on here," he muttered. "Human and nasty."

Strauss looked up to see Wiley standing outside the closed Brass Room door, Millie behind him, watching. Jerry beckoned him over.

"Someone is playing games with us, Wiley," he whispered in the man's ear. "Someone who knows what I can't explain. We need to get on with this." He looked at his watch, the one Farran had given him. "We've got one hour."

Wiley looked at Strauss. "Yes, sir. And at ten sharp, I'm taking you home for sleep."

Strauss met Wiley's eyes, but the younger officer did not waver. Christ, even his own officers felt they had to take care of him now. Jerry turned to Mildred. "Mrs. Keeps, if you would?"

Decidedly unhappy, Millie took a key out of her pocket and walked past them to the door of the Nursery Room. When the door swung open, the men heard a gruff voice say, "She's been here again, Millie. The girl. I saw her run past the door."

"Your door has been closed, Uncle Hugh." The woman's voice took on a softness Jerry didn't think she had. "You couldn't have seen anyone. There are two police officers who want to talk to you about Audrey, uncle. They won't stay long." She moved in to take the tray of breakfast things sitting beside his chair.

The man in the chair was very old. He sat with a military erectness, a blanket covering his legs. He wore a hearing aid in one ear that he kept turning up or down. No hair showed from under the Blue Jays baseball cap on his head, and his eyes were ferret-like—distorted by the Coke-bottle glasses on his nose.

With the echoes of the past around him, Jerry half expected to find Daniel Sterling sitting there despite his death years ago. But Hugh Keeps had a face—baby-fine skin, few wrinkles and not a whisker of stubble, but still a face with features instead of tortured skin.

"Mr. Keeps?" Strauss stuck out his hand. "I'm Inspector Jerry Strauss of the SD&G OPP and this is Detective Sergeant Jordan Wiley. We're here about the sudden death of Audrey Be—Audrey North last night."

The ferret eyes took a bead on him, ignoring the outstretched hand. "Bet you no one in this house is weeping over *that*," he said grimly.

"Why would you say that, sir?" asked Wiley.

"Audrey North was not loved," replied the old man quietly. "Not here and not anywhere else, either."

"Why not?"

"She made a living of cashing in on people's troubles," he muttered. "Probably a lot of folks wanted her dead."

"What exactly did she do, Mr. Keeps?" Jerry broke in. "Stan North says he didn't really keep tabs on her business deals. Just drove her around."

The old man snorted. "*That* little weasel? Hah! He was her chauffeur. Drove her around to all those business deals for years before they married. He knows what, who and where."

"You seem to know a lot about Stanley North," said Strauss.

"I know weasels," Hugh grunted. "Used to shoot them around the house as a boy."

"Were you good with a gun, Mr. Keeps?"

At Jerry's question, Wiley looked at him.

"Not bad," Hugh admitted. "But then weasels are stupid. Cunning little beggars, yes, but pretty damn stupid overall. Why? Audrey wasn't shot. She was stabbed."

"Now, Uncle Hugh," Millie warned, "Don't go getting yourself all worked up." She stood holding the breakfast tray, unwilling to leave them alone.

"You go on, Millie," said Hugh, not unkindly. "I'll talk to these fellas until you get back. Unless you'd rather send in that lady cop I've seen walking around," he added to Strauss. "Not hard to look at, is she?"

The weasel—Stan North—was sitting up with a coffee in the living room when Strauss and Wiley came back downstairs.

The interview with Hugh Keeps had not been overly helpful. The man had a regular bedtime of 9:00 p.m. Millie had brought him his hot chocolate at eight-thirty, helped him down the hall to the bathroom and then tucked him in for the night. He did not wear his hearing aid in bed, so could not have heard commotion in the hall or the Brass Room. He felt everyone at the B&B had a reason to kill Audrey, but couldn't offer any concrete examples.

"Except Stan North," Hugh finished. "If I were married to Audrey, I'd kill her, too. But then, he likes his money to gamble and he'd be killing the golden goose."

Strauss motioned to Constable Taylor who still stood sentry over Bradshaw.

"How much longer, Jurgen?" Bradshaw yawned and stretched. "Not that I mind spending time with the lovely Constable Taylor," he winked and grinned at her, "but the media conference beckons."

Taylor ignored him and joined Strauss, who turned to Bradshaw.

"Not long, Beauregard," he winked back at the man. "And the conference is later than planned. If you want to make it at all, I highly suggest that you don't move your ass from that chair while I talk to Constable Taylor. She won't be long, either."

The three officers convened in the office, door closed.

"Fifty bucks says Bradshaw has his ear to the den's swing door, trying to listen in," said Wiley.

"You're probably right," Taylor agreed, then smiled. "Would you excuse me for a moment, Inspector? I need something from the dining room."

Without making a sound, the young woman opened the office door and headed through the den. The men heard a thump followed by a muffled yelp.

"I'm so sorry, Mr. Bradshaw," came Taylor's voice loud and clear. "I didn't realize you were standing there. I need a pen."

They didn't catch the reply. After a moment, Taylor returned fighting a smile. She held up a pen.

"Got the pen, sir."

Strauss looked at Wiley and Wiley at Strauss.

"Is Mr. Bradshaw injured, Constable?" asked Strauss dryly.

"Not really, sir," came the deadpan reply. "But I might have given him a black eye."

There was a moment's silence, then Wiley coughed his smile into his hand.

Taylor flushed. "I mean . . . the man must be pushing *sixty*, for God's sake. I'm young enough to be his daughter and then some. Like get a reality check."

Strauss put his hand up. "Don't let him rattle you, Peg. That's what he's good at. Now," he looked at his watch. Nine-fifteen. "we have about forty-five minutes before we have to start letting people go. Wiley, I need backgrounds on all these people now. I still don't understand why everyone is here, at Sterling House. Bradshaw lives in the Ottawa area and could have driven down. The minister usually would travel five-star. The Norths have money and Stan likes to gamble. Why stay here when you could stay in a big hotel in Cornwall and be close to the casino in Akwesasne? The Norths strike me as a lot more flash than this. If any or all of them were here to meet someone, we have two choices: Mildred or Hugh Keeps. Which is it?

"Constable," he turned to Taylor, "Wiley has his cell phone off so that all calls go through me. You call in for the background checks and start with the Keeps, then the Norths. They're the dark horses here. I want to know if any connection exists at all."

"Wiley," Strauss added, "find out from North exactly what his wife did for a living. Don't take no for an answer. And find out why he's so tired this morning. I wonder if anyone gave him extra sleeping medication to make sure he didn't wake up while his wife was being murdered. That part of it bothers me, too."

Wiley left for the living room, but Taylor lingered. Strauss looked at her questioningly.

"I just wanted to ask you, sir . . . " she hesitated.

"Yes, Taylor?"

"Well, just now you . . . you called me 'Peg.' I'm Margaret, but no one calls me Peg. That's my mother's name." She stopped and waited for his reply.

Strauss slowly nodded. "Yes, I know. Your mother must have told you we knew each other in high school. Slip of the tongue." Jerry allowed himself a brief meander into another part of his past, his high school years and how he'd dated Peg Hoople right through to graduation. She'd been a lovely girl, inside and out. What had happened there? If they'd married, they would have had grown children by now. Maybe a daughter . . . He looked at Margaret and sighed. "Being back in this house isn't helping. And Bradshaw. I went to school with that bozo, too."

"Oh." She did the math. "I . . . I didn't mean that pushing sixty was really *old* or anything, sir . . . "

Again he cut her off.

"Leave it, Taylor. Call in for those backgrounds in here. I'm going out to speak to Mildred Keeps. Something her uncle said."

The kitchen was empty, the table cleared. Strauss stuck his head out into the garage. No one. He looked out to the road and saw Millie pulling two large garbage cans on wheels to the curb.

"Mrs. Keeps," he called out and walked out to join her. "I'm sorry," Jerry added as he came up. "You can't put out any garbage until the ident people go through this house. It's all evidence."

"You're kidding, right?" Millie protested as he began to wheel the cans back to the garage. "We have restrictions now, remember? I'm a business and I get only four bags a week. I'll lose a week."

"Mrs. Keeps," said Strauss over the noise of the wheels, "you said the Norths had been here before. How well did you know them?"

"Not well," Millie shrugged. "I get to know a little about all of my guests, but not the Norths overly much. As I said, Inspector, Audrey North was not a warm and fuzzy person."

"Did you know that Stan North likes to gamble?" Strauss faced off with her at the bottom of the stairs to the kitchen. "That seems kind of personal."

"Who told you that?" she asked warily.

"Your uncle. In fact, he not only knows about Stan's gambling habit, he also has a very strong opinion about the man. If you don't know them well, how does a man who barely leaves his room get that involved?"

Millie did not reply.

"Did your uncle get to know Stan North because he gambles, too? Or did?"

"What would that matter? It's legal."

"Some is. Some isn't. Did he have a gambling problem?"

"No," she looked away. "No."

"Did he borrow money from the Norths?"

"Of course not. Why would you think that?"

Jerry tapped the garbage can. "Because of the bank statements and cheques you were working on this earlier this morning. I thought it funny you would have the presence of mind to be doing paperwork with a dead body up in one of your guest rooms. For a B&B, it could mean ruin. And you were frightened all morning. But there you were, and I made a point of reading the names on the cheques. Learned to read upside down in high school. Helped out when you were standing in front of the principal's desk. The cheques, Mildred, were all made out to Audrey North. I'll bet they're all in here. Now, do I go ask Hugh to explain or do you save me the trouble?"

For a moment, Mildred said nothing. Then she slowly sat down on the bottom step.

"It wasn't my uncle who owed her. It was me."

"You?"

"Yes." She put her head in her hands. "I have a gambling problem. I racked up a lot of debt over the past few years. I'd gamble at the Thousand Islands casino so no one from here would know. That's where I met Stan North. At the tables. Audrey was there, too, but she never gambled. Just watched. Watched to see who lost and needed money.

"So, I borrowed a little from her when she offered. Then a little more. Then more. Then she hit me with the interest. It got out of control and that made me gamble more. Finally, I was in so deep she began to threaten me. That's when I told my uncle. He had no money. All of it went into buying this house. Audrey finally said she would take Sterling House in lieu of my debt, and I would be paid in full. I tried everything to find new financing, but couldn't get enough. Audrey was going to close on the deal this weekend."

She looked up at Strauss. "Audrey said we would stay here, running the place for now. At least me. She said she had no truck with supporting a sick old man. That it was time for Hugh to go into a home. I couldn't let her do that, Inspector. It would have killed him."

"So you killed her with the old knife."

"No." Millie shook her head slowly. "No. I did not kill Audrey North. But," the little woman rose defiantly to face Jerry, "I, for one, am damn glad she's dead. Just plain nasty."

Millie marched up the stairs and vanished into the kitchen. Jerry stood thoughtfully in the garage for a moment. He looked around at what had replaced the old back porch on the house when it resided in Wales.

Moneylending. Extortion.

I'm in trouble, Jerry. Possibly big trouble. And you're the only one who can help me.

Blackmail? And the thought of Bella's statement, that he had a son out there somewhere. A son. Not a could have, like with Peg Hoople. But a did. How could she have dropped a bombshell like that? Here? And would she have ever told him if it weren't to save her own hide?

What would life be like if he did have a child after all?

Strauss strode out into the garden area, past the pool. Here he had privacy and quiet. And there was a hammock . . .

Eyeing the hammock covetously, Jerry pulled a card out of his pocket and checked the number before punching it in.

"Lynnie?" he asked when she picked up.

"Oh, no. No you don't, Strauss," came the reply. "No sucking up now that you've kicked me out and earned the ire of the media."

"Lynnie," he said in a low voice. "This is serious. You were right this morning. This is about that Audrey and it is weird. I need your help."

"I meant the front porch was weird."

"The front porch?"

"Yes. It looks exactly the same as it used to in Wales, remember?"

"I remember, but that's not what's weird." He took a deep breath and let it out. "Lynnie, I need backgrounds on a few people, ASAP. Unofficial ones." He gave her names and details. "These people are dark horses. Isabella Roberts is . . . " he chose his word carefully, "pretty well-known, as is Bradshaw. But the Norths and the Keeps are unknown quantities to me. I can't explain the whole thing yet, Lynn, but something about this murder connects back to that summer Joe Beckett was killed."

"*What*? That happened almost fifty years ago. Hey, wait a minute. What murder? Is that the Audrey that's 'cooling off' as Buck put it?"

"Yes. I didn't answer you this morning when you asked me if it was *that* Audrey. It is. Or was. Audrey North was Audrey Beckett in Wales."

There was absolute silence for a minute.

"Audrey Beckett again," came Lynn voice finally. "And now someone's killed her."

"Lynn," Strauss sighed, "this is absolutely between us for now. There's something else."

"Okay." The old friendship from adolescence kicked in. "What is it?"

"Joe Beckett was found with his hunting rifle, but it was a stab wound to the chest that killed him, remember? Well, Audrey was killed with the knife they thought was used on Joe."

"The Granny Hoople knife? But that's impossible. It disappeared that night. They never found it."

"Exactly." Strauss fell silent.

"Jerry," said Lynn slowly. "Be careful. Be very careful. This feels weird, yes, but also . . . *personal*. To you. I don't like it. I don't like it at all."

"Are you suggesting that this was all staged to give me a rough time?" Staged. The word struck a chord.

"I don't know. That sounds insane, but the word 'weird' here is becoming more than a little small."

"Then get me those lives. Especially Audrey. She's the key. I know who Audrey Beckett was. I want to know who she had become. And if the old man is right—that everyone in this house had a reason to kill her."

"Including the minister?" Lynn probed.

I'm in trouble, Jerry . . .

"No comment, Holmes," he said briskly. "But I can't see her risking everything for murder. Or Bradshaw either. He's an asshole, but that's as far as it goes there."

"Except about his mother, remember."

"His mother?"

"Yes. His parents split up around the time of the murder. It came out in the investigation that Rowdy had been having an affair with Audrey. He was even considered a suspect for a bit, until they arrested Daniel Sterling. The Bradshaws separated and Buck left with his mother for St. Catharines. About six months later, she died and he came back to live with his dad."

"I remember all that," Strauss agreed, "and how Buck used to have a thing for you in our Osnabruck District High School days." The dig was met with silence. Jerry allowed himself a silent grin. "Still, his father's affair was long ago and Buck was a kid. What's the connection to Audrey's murder?"

"Maybe revenge for his mother's death," Lynn offered. "Those wounds run deep, as you know. And his father died just last year."

"Beryl Bradshaw died of pneumonia," said Jerry. "What would Audrey have to do with that?"

"That's what they put on the death certificate, and it was the story Buck and his dad told. They used to hide things like that in those days. But remember, Jerry, my cousin was Meredith Murphy. And what Meredith didn't know about people's private lives around here wasn't worth knowing."

"Are you saying that Audrey Beckett killed Beryl Bradshaw?"

"In a manner of speaking. Beryl Bradshaw died of a broken heart."

"And the pneumonia finished her off?"

"Nope. Beryl killed herself. And from what I remember of Meredith's story, Buck was the one who found her."

Chapter 9: Interregnum Two

OTTAWA 9:30 a.m.

"This is just crazy, Michelle. It doesn't make sense."

I was on my cell phone, barrelling down Highway 31 out of Ottawa south to Morrisburg. The plane had landed an hour ago and I was finally free to head home. I'd called Michelle immediately on landing and the update wasn't good. Still no Diana, still no word. Michelle had called her husband and then called me back.

"I tried Jordan on his cell, but he's not picking up," said Michelle. "I called the office and he's out on a call somewhere. They're looking for him, too. I have April here going over Diana's computer and e-mail."

"Why?"

"I was afraid she was hanging out overnight with Ryan, but it's someone else. Someone I don't know. None of her friends have seen her. God, Farran, what if she's gone to meet some creep from a chat room?"

The woman's voice broke. I passed the Gloucester police station and instinctively slowed down. For a minute.

"Michelle," I said firmly, "she wouldn't do that. She's too smart to do anything that stupid."

"They all think they're too smart. That's why they disappear."

"We'll find her. I'll be there in about forty minutes if I don't get stopped. I'll call Jerry next, see if he knows where Jordan is. If not, he'll know what to do. Listen," I added, "let me talk to April."

My phone beeped. Low battery. A moment later, a tearful voice came on.

"April, it's Farran Mackenzie. I'm a friend of Diana. I want you to tell me exactly what she said before she left last night. Word for word."

There was some sniffling, then the voice returned a little stronger.

"Diana said she was going to go out for a couple of hours. That she would be back around midnight. I was going to wait up for her, but we'd had a soccer tournament yesterday and I was bagged. I fell asleep . . . " The voice quavered.

"You couldn't know things would go wrong," I soothed. If this kid were mine . . . "Now relax and try to remember what she told you. Who was she going to meet?"

"Harry."

"Harry? Had she mentioned him before this?"

"No. Just last night. She seemed excited about meeting him." Sniffles and a throat clearing.

"Why? What did she say?"

"Well, she talked silly. Didn't really make sense."

"In what way?" Another beep.

"I don't know. Something about his smell."

I wanted to reach into the phone and shake this girl. "Try to remember exactly—"

"Not smell. Scent. Scent! *That's* it." April shouted.

"Scent?" Now she'd totally lost me.

"Yes. That was it. It was really weird the way she put it. That's why I thought she was so excited." April took a breath. "She said, 'I'm on the scent of Harry and I'll make contact tonight.' What did she mean, Mrs. Mackenzie?"

I thought for a moment. "I haven't a clue," I admitted. "It didn't mean anything to you?"

"No. That's why I'm going through her computer. I thought it might be a user name or password or something."

"Good idea. Let me talk to Mrs. Wiley again."

When Michelle came on, I told her I would call Jerry and get back to her. Then I clicked off, but before I could punch in Jerry's number, the phone rang.

"Farran?"

"Lynn? I didn't recognize your number."

"New one. Listen, I've been trying to get you for the past couple of days."

"My reception comes and goes Down East. Lynn," I changed the subject, "where are you right now?"

"In Ingleside. Skulking, so Jerry won't see me."

"Why? What's going on with him?"

"He's holed up at Sterling House with a dead woman he used to know from Wales."

"The B&B? Okay, I'll bite, Holmes. Is he stuck for a date 'cause I'm AWOL?"

She had to laugh at that. "No. This is weird, even for Jerry." She proceeded to fill me in on the little reunion going on in the

B&B. "And the minister of Canadian Heritage is there as well, right in the middle of it."

"Poor Jerry."

"Yes. It's not good. I have a bad feeling about this. Personally," she added, "he's dealing with a lot more than a blast from the past. That summer, Jerry had already lost his dad in the fire and then your dad when he left on the ship. The two men in his life had gone. I think Jerry had quite the hole in his life, and that's why his mother had him help out at the Sterling place. It was more than a summer job."

"And did it work out that way?"

"I think it did at first. Sterling was a recluse and the neighbourhood kids were afraid of him because of his disfigured face. But Jerry seemed very comfortable there the few times I saw him. And then Sterling was arrested and taken away for murder.

"Another father figure MIA," I mused. That reminded me of Diana. "Lynn, we've got a problem. Diana Wiley is missing and we can't find Jordan to tell him. Is he with Jerry?"

"Yes, he is. Missing? What happened?"

"She went to a girlfriend's place last night and then took off, first saying she was hunting ghosts but talking about some guy named Harry and his scent—"

Sterling House. Something in the back of my mind clicked.

"Shit!" I cried. I slammed on the brakes and pulled recklessly off the highway into the gravel, almost going for a rollover and causing all my papers and notebooks in the front passenger seat to hit the floor. Horns honked around and then past me, but I didn't look up.

"What's wrong, Farran?" Lynn's voice came from the cell in my lap. "And I still need to tell you my news . . . "

I picked up the cell. "Hang on, Lynn. I need to check something." I put the cell in my cupholder and began to dig through the mess in the floorspace. My phone beeped ominously.

"Farran?" came the voice from the cupholder. "What the hell are you doing? Are you all right?"

I pulled a red notebook out triumphantly and frantically began to leaf through it. S. Sterling House. Please let me be wrong.

"There it is," I said to the car. I read the entry and my heart sank. It had now been over twelve hours since Diana had left April's house.

"Farran?" Two beeps. Damn phone.

"Lynn? I think I know where Diana is. You have to tell them."

Two more beeps. The low battery sign took over from call display. My voice went flat against the phone, but there was still power. I couldn't hear Lynn anymore, but she might still hear me.

"Lynn, if you can hear me, listen. Get to Jerry and tell him about Diana. It's her, not a boy. Harry," I babbled, "Harry is short for Harriet. Harriet Sterling. The legend is that when she appears, you smell a strong scent of violets. Her favourite flower. She was picking them when she fell and drowned. Diana was being clever. That's what she meant by being on the scent of Harry."

I thought of Audrey Beckett dead and Jerry cloistered with a nasty group of people, one a desperate murderer. The place was crawling with suspects and cops. If I were right, why the hell hadn't we heard from Diana? I suddenly felt cold all over.

"Lynn," I repeated, "get to Jerry. Break the door down if you have to and tell him. Tell him she's there. She's *there*."

The phone beeped again and flickered.

"Lynn" I screamed into the dying instrument, "Diana is somewhere *inside Sterling House*."

The phone gave a death beep and went black.

Chapter 10: Doors

Strauss took the stairs two at a time and stopped for a breather outside the Blue Room door. Then he pounded on it.

"Bradshaw," he barked, "we need to talk."

Buck opened the door, holding an ice pack to one eye. His suitcase was open on the bed. For the first time, Jerry noticed—with a small grain of satisfaction—that Buck was succumbing to the advances of middle-age spread.

"Always a pleasure, Jurgen," Buck said with a grin, then winced. "Ooh. Your lovely constable packs a punch with a door. I'm wondering if I should consider charges of police misconduct."

Strauss closed the door and faced him. "I'm still wondering why you're here."

"Told you. To get cozy with Roberts. Not that I've been having any luck with you standing in my way."

"Since when would that slow you down? Except for a few tries when I've been watching, you haven't made any real effort to speak to Isabella Roberts." He quietly picked up a bottle of sleeping medication on the night stand and set it back down. "You didn't come here to talk to her. You came to see Audrey North."

Bradshaw tossed the icebag on the bed and finished his packing.

"Why would I want to see Audrey?" he asked over his shoulder.

"Because with her recent move into political circles, you'd met her or seen her photograph on the wire and realized who she was. Maybe you started looking for her after your father died, as unfinished business. Maybe you've been tracking her for a while, and this shindig, with the minister coming and everyone in Sterling House, was too good a chance to pass up."

Buck shrugged and did not turn around. "Sounds like a lot of work to meet up with someone I barely knew as a kid in Wales."

"But she knew you, Buck. At least, she knew your father. Too well, as I recall." Strauss saw Bradshaw's shoulders stiffen. "And your parents' marriage didn't survive it. Nor did your mother."

Buck stood motionless, his back to Jerry.

"Leave my mother out of this, Strauss," came the warning reply.

Jerry moved closer to Buck. "Your mother committed suicide because she couldn't deal with the loss of her marriage," he said softly. "And you found her. I can't imagine what that would feel like, but I can understand your wanting Audrey Beckett dead."

Bradshaw whirled around and grabbed Jerry by the shirt, slamming him up against the wall.

"Yes, you can't imagine what that was like," he said, inches from Jerry's face. "Or what it's like to live with that all these years. Or how much I wanted revenge on Audrey Beckett." He released Jerry's shirt from his grasp. "But I didn't kill her. And I do owe whoever did."

"Is that your story, Buck?" Jerry looked him in the eye. "It's a big load to carry, especially for a child."

"You have no idea."

"Yes, I do," Strauss replied quietly. "My father was left to burn in the sawmill fire back in Aultsville. He'd just been diagnosed with ALS by Doc Burns. He killed himself. The person who found him set the fire to make it look like murder."

Buck stared at him, silent.

"I never knew until two years ago," Jerry continued. "It's been a lot to deal with and I'm an adult. It would be an inhuman burden on a child."

Bradshaw didn't reply. He looked at Jerry for a minute, then slowly sat down on the bed.

"You keep wondering how they could do it," he said finally. "Leave you, I mean. You keep wondering why you weren't worth sticking around for. Or if there was something you should have done for them, that would have helped. Right?" Buck looked up at Jerry who nodded, then down at his hands. "My dad and I never spoke about it. It was, I guess, the only way he could deal with it. He didn't think that maybe I needed something different." He looked up at Jerry. "You've only known a couple of years. How did you find out?"

"It came out after Hal Leonard's body was found. It was never made public as part of the investigation because it had no bearing on it. There are only a few people who know."

"That must have been a shock."

"It was. I always had a hard time believing Hal Leonard had killed my father, but I more or less went along with the gossip." Strauss closed his eyes. They burned, like the guilt in his chest.

"You were just a kid," said Buck. "How the hell could you ever get a handle on something like that?"

Strauss opened his eyes and looked at Bradshaw. "Buck, your father died last year?"

Buck nodded.

"Heart attack," he said simply.

"Then all the players are dead and I need a straight answer. Did your father kill Joe Beckett over Audrey?"

Buck shook his head slowly. "No. I know that's what they thought for a bit before they settled on Sterling, but I never believed it. I knew my dad. He was obsessed with Audrey and could make a mistake, like being with her, but he wasn't a killer." Buck looked up at Jerry. "Neither am I, Strauss."

"Then I'll ask you one more time. Why are you here?"

Bradshaw took in a deep breath and let it go. "I guess with Audrey dead, my deadline has changed a bit."

"So you did come to see her?"

"I did. But not to kill her." He rose and scooped out the clothes in his suitcase. Then he took a penknife from his pocket and peeled open a false bottom underneath. There was a slim tan envelope inside and he handed it to Strauss. "If you confiscate this, it doesn't matter. These are only copies and the originals are safely out of the way. I was about to do an exposé on Audrey North and her very shady activities. They involved loansharking, extortion and kickbacks from brokering contracts. Including some direct ties to people on Parliament Hill. She'd come a long way from being the Black Widow of Wales."

Strauss took the envelope. "What did you want from Audrey? A pay-off?"

Bradshaw shrugged. "I'm not sure how I was going to play it. But I did want to make sure she knew it was from me and who I was. Who my parents had been. I wanted her to know it was payback time."

"You said ties to people on Parliament Hill," Jerry said slowly. "Were any of them to Isabella Roberts?"

As he opened the door to the Blue Room, Jerry could have sworn he heard the Nursery Room door click shut.

Another door. The Gold Room.

It opened immediately and Bella stood there, dressed for the media conference. She looked at her watch.

"Matt will be back here shortly," she said. "I was just coming to find you."

Strauss entered the room and closed the door.

"I have one question for you."

"Have you thought about helping me, Jerry?" she cut in. "I know it was a bombshell to drop on you like that but—"

He put up his hand to cut her off.

"I'm not going there. At least not right now. There's a dead woman in the next room, and right about now Wiley is calling it in. The identification team will be here within the hour. And that's when it all goes out of my hands. I need a straight answer from you. You said someone was digging around and was going to make your affair with Michael Browning public knowledge. Establish possible ties to organized crime. Was that person Buck Bradshaw?"

Bella looked at him for a minute, at the envelope in his hand, then turned and walked to the window. She pulled the sheers back to see the street.

"It's a nice little community, isn't it Jerry? Maybe we should have just married and settled down to a quiet life somewhere like this."

"You didn't answer my question."

She was silent for several minutes. Jerry didn't budge. Finally, Bella said over her shoulder, "Yes. It was Buck Bradshaw. He's been at me for some time now. My aides have stonewalled him, but then he turned up here and all I could do was avoid him as best I could."

"Are you sure about that?"

"I just said so." She dropped the curtain and turned to him, then turned back to the window. "There's some woman with curly hair running up the front sidewalk. I think she was out in the hall with everyone this morning."

The words were barely out of her mouth when they both heard the sound of someone hammering on the front door.

"Jerry! Jerry!" came the muffled words. "Open up! It's an emergency!"

Strauss didn't blink.

"Are you willing to make a statement that it was Bradshaw?" he persisted.

"Yes. Aren't you going to see what she wants?"

Strauss turned and opened the door to leave. "Stay here and stay locked until I tell you different." Then he shut the door.

The girl turned to the other.

"I think it is safe now for you to leave. Move quietly and go down to the front door."

The little door slowly swung open, bringing the sunlight into the small, dark space. The other carefully got up and, blinking, stepped out into the hall.

"Thank you," said the other to the girl.

But the small dark space was empty.

Lynn bulldozed over Mildred Keeps—no small feat—and straight through into Jerry Strauss as he reached the front foyer.

"Lynn, what the hell—"

"Jerry, it's important. Can I talk to you alone—with Jordan Wiley?"

Wiley stood in the living room, where he had followed Mildred to the door. Strauss looked at his old schoolchum, saw the urgency in her face and nodded to Wiley. "Okay, let's take it to the kitchen. Taylor, keep an eye on things."

As they moved to the kitchen, Strauss added, "Did you call in yet?"

"Yes, sir. They'll be here in thirty minutes." His cell phone rang and he looked at it. "Message, Inspector."

"See what it is and join us."

When the kitchen door had swung shut, Strauss glared at Lynn. She, in turn, looked him dead in the eye.

"I got a call from Farran this morning. She said Diana Wiley is missing. Went AWOL from a friend's house during a sleepover yesterday. They called Michelle early this morning when the friend woke up and found Diana hadn't come back, then spent time calling all her friends but no luck. That's when Michelle tried to call Jordan, but his cell phone was off and dispatch couldn't reach him here. No service."

Jerry went white. *I need time. Not much. Just a couple of hours, tops. Wait to call ident. I don't want a flurry of uniforms in here and outside. Let's say it's to protect the minister until the banquet tonight. Turn off your cell phone and all calls will go through me . . .* He'd done it again. If anything had happened to Diana Wiley—

Jordan burst through the swing door and grabbed Jerry's arm. "Inspector, my daughter—"

"I know." Jerry turned heavily to Wiley. "That's why Lynn is here. We'll find her. Go to Michelle and I'll hold the fort here till ident comes."

"Wait!" Lynn put out her hands. "You don't understand. She's here. Farran says she's here."

"Diana?" asked Jordan incredulously. "In Sterling House?"

"Can't be," Jerry said flatly. "We've been here since dawn. We would have seen her or Mildred would've . . . " His voice died off and they all fell silent with understanding. "Why does Farran think she's here? And how did she get in this? She's Down East."

"She's on her way home. Michelle called her because Diana told her friend before she left that she was going ghosthunting and that's what she was researching with Farran." Lynn put her fingers to her temples and closed her eyes. "Let me try to remember. Farran was going on about someone and then her phone cut out." She opened her eyes. "Harry. That's it. Harry is a ghost that haunts Sterling House. Diana is somewhere in this house and has been since last night."

The two cops looked at each other.

"Farran Mackenzie might have a screw loose sometimes," said Strauss gravely, "but if she says Diana is here, then Diana is somewhere in this house."

Wiley swallowed. "Then why haven't we—"

"She may be sleeping," Jerry cut off the thought. "She might be injured and unable to call out. In any rate, we search this house again from top to bottom. The main floor is open, except for the front hall closet. I'll do that and the upstairs. Jordan, you check the basement again and then do the garage and the garden. Lynn, I want you to stay with the others in the living room."

They moved out, Lynn on Strauss's heels. "The hell I will," she muttered to Jerry's back.

"Taylor," Strauss yelled as he crossed the dining room, "get everyone into the living room. Ministers of tourism, tabloid journalists and even very old men. We have a missing person who may be on the premises, hiding or injured and unable to call for help."

Stan North and Mildred Keeps got to their feet.

"That's impossible," Millie spluttered, but then her face cleared. "My uncle said . . . "

"Said what?" Strauss wheeled around to face her.

"He said he saw someone who shouldn't be here," she said slowly. "A girl. I thought he was dreaming or thinking of our ghost story. I didn't take him seriously."

"That means she's upstairs." Strauss headed to the second floor with Lynn and Taylor in tow. The constable stopped at the Blue Room to knock as the other two made their way down the hall.

Buck opened the door. "Constable Taylor," he leered. "I'd invite you in, but I have to leave for the media conference."

Taylor considered giving him another eye to match the first but thought better of it.

"The inspector wants everyone downstairs in the living room. That includes you, lover boy."

Bella opened her door as Jerry approached.

"What's going on? Is Matt here?"

"No, but I need everyone downstairs. Living room. You, too, Bella."

She looked at him and then wordlessly walked down the hall to where Taylor was waiting at the top of the stairs.

Strauss turned to Lynn.

"I just hope to God that girl isn't in the Brass Room with a corpse."

"I just hope she's all right," Lynn replied. "Where do we start?"

Jerry didn't answer.

"Jerry?"

He put a finger to his lips and then pointed down the little hallway that led to the sitting room. The sitting room door was closed. Catlike, the man walked down the hall past the two bookcases and up to the door. He tried the knob slowly and the door opened.

In the corner on a chair sat a girl in a white dress, knees up, head down. The smell of violets hit him and he felt his heart pound.

"Diana?" he called softly.

"Uncle Jerry?" came a voice from his right. He turned and saw Diana kneeling on a chair in the far corner, next to the window of the Brass Room. Her face was white and tear-stained. "Is that someone dead in there?"

Strauss turned to Lynn.

"Get Jordan up here."

"Already on it," Lynn replied as she headed to the stairs.

"Diana," he added to the girl, "your mother is half crazy about you. And who is . . . " His voice trailed off as he looked around the room. The girl in white was gone.

Diana got down off the chair. "Did you see her?" she asked Jerry. "Did you see Harriet?"

Jerry didn't reply. Then he took the girl by the arm.

"Why didn't we see you in here before?"

"Because she hid me. To keep me safe, she said."

Strauss didn't ask who.

"Where? And why to keep you safe? From what?"

"From death," said Diana. "Harriet said that death had come to the house again. Has it?"

"Yes, it has. Now where were you?"

"Down here." Diana led him out of the sitting room to one of the bookshelves in the hallway. "I was here before ten. I slipped in through the garage before Mrs. Keeps locked everything up and came up here. Everyone's doors were closed, so I hid in the sitting room with the light off. Then I saw Harriet, and she told me to hide in here." Diana felt under one of the shelves and Jerry heard a small click. Then the bookcase swung slowly out into the hall, revealing a small cubbyhole behind. Strauss stepped into it.

"What the hell?" said a voice. "Diana?"

"Daddy!"

The girl ran into Wiley's arms and they held each other close. Wiley put his head on hers for a moment, silently. Then he held her out at arm's length.

"Di," he said shakily, "you're grounded for the rest of your life. I'm going to call your mother and let her know you're all right. But," he added, turning to Strauss who had stepped back into the hall, "what is this? A secret door?"

"This backs on to the Brass Room," Jerry said pointedly. "This could," he added with a smile, "literally be the opening we've been looking for."

"How do you mean?" Lynn came up behind Wiley.

"Lynnie," Strauss replied, "when we talked earlier, the idea came up that this whole thing has been staged. That's stuck with me all morning. Diana," he added to the girl. "when you were in the hiding place, could you hear what went on in the hallway or the rooms?"

Diana nodded. "The hallway and the room behind."

"Tell me what you heard last night."

She told him. He listened, nodding slowly.

"That makes sense." Jerry turned to his old friend. "Lynn, did you get any scoop for me on these people?"

"Well," she said, "I've just started with Audrey, as you asked. I'm still waiting to hear from a friend in the business, but I did talk to an old family friend about her years in Ingleside."

"And?"

"And it was brief. And weird. Seems she rented a house in the village for a year, and went around telling everyone about the big house she was going to build. But she never did. One day, Audrey was gone. Word was she went to the West Coast."

Strauss thought about it for a moment. It wouldn't have been like Audrey to brag and not follow through. Showing off was her favourite pastime, if he remembered correctly. Strange. Something had happened.

"Okay, Wiley. Let Diana call your wife. Join me in a few minutes. I'm going to hear what Taylor was able to dig up on our friends downstairs and then the show begins."

"The show, sir?" echoed Wiley.

"The show," Strauss confirmed grimly. "This whole thing was staged. Acts One and Two have gone according to plan. What the others don't know is that Act Three is about to begin—but this time we're writing the script."

Chapter 11: Locks

"I've called you all here in the living room to unmask a killer," said Jerry dramatically. "Mr. North, you will be happy to hear that we know who murdered your wife."

"We're not all here," Buck pointed out dryly from the corner wingback chair, legs flung out on the floor. "The old guy is still in his room."

"He's asleep," Constable Taylor explained. "I didn't want to wake him up."

"Are you sure he's not dead, too?" Stan North asked tremulously from the davenport.

"He has a nap every morning at this time," Mildred snapped. She stood in front of the fireplace, arms crossed. "Usually, while I clean the rooms. Besides, he didn't have anything to do with this."

"So you keep insisting, Mrs. Keeps," Jerry said, "yet something has really shaken you. You, a woman who can look over a murdered corpse like a menu."

Millie flushed and fell silent.

Isabella Roberts, from her seat beside Stan, looked up at her curiously.

They had been waiting for Jerry when he emerged from a quick huddle with Taylor and Wiley in the kitchen.

"No big surprises, Inspector," the constable had sighed. "Hugh Keeps is Mildred's uncle through marriage. He moved from a nursing home in Grimsby to live with her here when she bought this place. He's ninety-four, served in World War II in the navy and has no record. He is legally blind. Mildred is Mildred Storm Keeps. Her husband died over ten years ago. She's a retired registered nurse and the current owner of Sterling House. No police record either. Stan North is American. Former marine, weapons specialist. Then bodyguard. Then Mr. Audrey North. That's when he disappeared from the radar. For the last two years, nothing. Retired into married life, I guess. Skimmed the edges of the casino life in New York state. No offences, but hung out with certain well-known undesirables, along with his wife.

Racked up considerable debt and has been barred from several casinos for the time being. Except for the past three months. No sign of him crossing the border.

"The big dark horse is Audrey North," she continued. "Audrey North, born Audrey Connelly. Married Joseph Beckett in 1947. Widowed ten years later when he was murdered in Wales. She disappeared for a number of years after that, but popped up in the sixties in Vancouver. Seemed to make very good money with various innocent business ventures. She's been fingered for moneylending, embezzlement and fraud, but always managed to leave others holding the bag. Charges were laid once for extortion but later dropped."

"Grimsby," Strauss had muttered. He fell silent, thinking. Then rubbed his eyes and glanced at his watch. Nine-forty-five. Fifteen minutes till The Suit returned for Bella, nostrils flaring.

"Okay," he snapped to. "Thanks, Taylor. Now let's get this show on the road."

And they now sat expectantly in the living room. Strauss looked at them all. Let the games begin, people.

"Hugh Keeps said something this morning that stuck with me," Jerry began. "He said that everyone in this house last night had a reason to want Audrey North dead." Strauss paused for effect. "Counting Hugh himself," he continued, "I now agree.

"In 1957, a man named Joe Beckett was murdered in this house. Stabbed once through the heart with an heirloom knife that was missing and never found. He was found with his hunting rifle and they figured he'd been waiting to surprise Daniel Sterling in a tryst with Mrs. Beckett. Beckett's widow was Audrey North. And the knife that killed him is the one in Audrey's chest upstairs."

"My God, Jerry." Bella put a hand to her mouth.

"God's got nothing to do with this, Bella," Jerry replied grimly. "This is all human design—very human and very nasty. And weird. Lynn Holmes said the situation was weird and the label fit. Weird because of the history and weird because it all seemed to be alive again. Seemed, that is, because that's what the killer wanted."

The group in front of him was dead silent. Constable Taylor stood with Sergeant Wiley behind Strauss in the dining room.

"So, assuming the knife was used not only to kill Audrey but also to establish a possible connection to Joe Beckett's murder, that leaves us with several points to identify our murderer. First,"

Jerry held up one finger, "the killer had to *know* about the murder here in the past and Audrey's connection to it. Perhaps also mine. Second, the murderer had to have access to the knife. That's problematic until we find out where the hell it's been for fifty years. Mrs. Keeps says she's never seen it before, so it wasn't displayed in the house. At least, that's her story. Third, the killer had to have access to Audrey herself late last night.

"Mr. North," Jerry turned to Stan, "was your door locked when you went to bed?"

"I locked it, but . . . but Audrey went to the bathroom after I was in bed," he replied. "I don't know if she locked it again. Probably not. She wasn't as big on security as I was." The man fell silent.

"And you take sleeping pills every night?"

"Yes. Both Audrey and I do. Why?"

"The rooms upstairs share a bathroom. Where did you and your wife keep your medication?"

North shrugged. "On the dresser in the bedroom."

"Available to anyone who wanted to have you take more last night so you would sleep through an intruder coming into your room—and Audrey through being attacked."

North looked at Strauss. "That's why I'm so sleepy this morning? But how would they do it?"

"By putting some in your food," Jerry replied quietly.

"My food? But we ate here last night . . . " North turned to look at Mildred.

The woman stood up. "Are you suggesting—"

"I am looking at the possibilities," Strauss said crisply. "How did you serve supper last night, Mrs. Keeps? On trays to the rooms?"

She blinked.

"Well, yes." Millie slowly sat down again.

"In what order were they served?"

"Uh, well . . . I started with Mrs. Roberts, her being the minister and all. Then I served Mr. Bradshaw. He offered to help me with the other trays, but I said no. Then I brought up the Norths' meal."

"On one tray or in two trips?"

"One tray. They weren't having dessert."

"And in each case, did you leave the tray on the hall table to knock on the door?"

"Yes."

"With the Norths' tray, how long did it sit there?"

"For a few minutes. I went in and we . . . " She flushed and looked at Strauss. "We chatted a bit. Then I went out and brought the tray in."

"So it sat there unattended for a few minutes in the hall?"

"Hey," Bradshaw sat up. "What are you implying, Jurgen?"

"Possibilities, Beauregard. Only possibilities." Jerry looked over his shoulder at the staircase to the second floor and then turned back to the group in the living room. "Our killer had to have access to the Norths' supper to lace it with sleeping medication. Every one of you has some form of sleeping pill in your room, with the exception of Hugh Keeps. But he would have access to yours, Mildred."

She opened her mouth, then closed it again.

"Next," Jerry continued, "our killer needed access to the Brass Room that night. In terms of that, Mildred Keeps has a key. Hugh Keeps also knows where that key is."

"He didn't do it!" Millie stood up, her apron clenched in a fist. "He couldn't hurt anybody."

Strauss turned on her. "Then why do you think he did?"

Everyone looked at Mildred, who said nothing. Then she slowly sat down again.

"You said your uncle spoke of seeing a girl in the house who shouldn't be here," said Strauss. "That was last night, wasn't it? He saw her because he was out in the hallway and you saw him there."

"He was just wandering," Millie whispered. "He does that now and then. I went out to the bathroom and he was standing in the hallway near the Brass Room, just at the corner where the hall goes out to the sitting room. I put him back to bed." She looked up at Strauss. "He wouldn't hurt a fly."

"He might, if that fly was hurting you. That brings us to motive. Our killer needs a motive. Hugh Keeps feels that everyone staying here had reason to want Audrey dead. Interesting hypothesis for a man who barely leaves his room, but it is still one worth considering. And he may be right." Jerry gazed at each of them in turn. "Audrey North had a long history of taking no prisoners in her life. Mildred, Audrey was going to take this house away from you. That covers both you and your uncle. Buck, we talked about the damage the woman did to your family when you were a boy. Sometimes wounds that deep don't heal—without closure. Bella, you said that someone was building a smear campaign on you with circumstantial details from your life. When I asked if it were Buck Bradshaw, you jumped at the suggestion." Buck stood up, but Jerry waved him down. "I don't buy it. As much as Buck writes creative fiction sometimes, smear campaigns are not his style. It was Audrey, and she was pressuring you for her own political interests. And your staying here makes sense if you were looking for access to Audrey."

Isabella said nothing, her face like stone.

"So," Jerry smiled at them, "we all have motives. Even Mr. North, who might just have been getting tired of being married.

"The last detail," he continued, "is the history of the murder in this house. Someone used it for a purpose last night. Used it for stage effect, to draw attention to the past and away from the present. Somehow, Bradshaw, that backfires in your case, but maybe you needed to do that to have the last say with Audrey Beckett. But you do know all about that summer, and the murder of Joe Beckett because you were there. So was Audrey, which means Stan North probably knows all about it, too. Isabella Roberts knows because I told her years ago. And both Millie and Hugh Keeps might know through researching the history of this house. In this, too, we have a level playing field. Except for the tricky question of where was the knife for fifty years?

"And we might have remained stuck on that one point except for one thing. A cameo appearance the killer didn't bargain for." Jerry walked over to the stairs. "Ladies and gentlemen, I bring your attention to the curious incident of the dog in the night. Lynn?" he called.

Lynn Holmes came down the stairs, a slim blonde girl behind her. Everyone in the living room stood up.

"Where did *she* come from?" Stan asked.

"How did she get in my house?" said Millie.

Lynn led Diana to Strauss and then stood over by Bradshaw.

"This," Jerry replied, "is Diana." He purposely omitted her last name, shooting a look at Wiley. "Diana is an amateur ghost hunter. She snuck in here last night before Mildred locked up to stake out the ghost of Harriet Sterling, and has been here ever since. Most importantly, Diana spent the night awake in a hidden cubbyhole in the upstairs hallway. A position that didn't allow her to see anything, but did give her full hearing rights to all action upstairs. Diana," he turned to the girl, "I want you to tell everyone what you heard from inside the cubbyhole last night."

Out of the corner of his eye, Strauss saw everybody stiffen. All but one.

Diana licked her lips nervously. "Well," she began, "at first it was quiet. I heard someone walk up the stairs and go through to the far end of the hall. Then a door opened across from me and someone was moving around in the hallway as though they were looking for something. The door at the end of the hall opened and I heard a woman's voice speak to the other person. They walked away together and I heard a door close. Then the woman used the bathroom and went back to bed."

Millie nodded as though to herself.

"After that, someone came out of the room right behind me and went into the bathroom. I heard the bathtub start to run. While that person had a bath, three people came in turn to the room behind me and spoke to the woman inside."

"Spoke?" Jerry asked. "Could you hear what about?"

"Well, they argued, actually. All three. Two women and a man. A woman came first and was angry about some rumours or a story about her or something. A little bit after she left, a man came and talked very low. I couldn't catch it. But it was an argument, too. And the woman inside the room laughed at him."

Isabella looked at the floor. Buck flushed and turned away.

"Then the woman in the room at the end of the hall came out and went in to speak to the other woman in the room. That argument was pretty heated. They kept their voices low, I guess because people were supposed to be sleeping, but I could tell they were both angry. Then the woman left. The person in the bathroom let the water out and went back into the room behind me. Then it was quiet again."

Diana stopped and looked up at Strauss. He looked at her for a moment and nodded. Then he prompted, "Then what? Tell us exactly what you heard over the course of the night."

Diana hesitated. "Exactly?" she said.

"Yes," Jerry replied. "Exactly. A woman has been murdered, Diana. Think carefully and don't leave anything out."

The girl looked at him for a moment with a question in her eyes. She gazed around at the people in the living room and over to where her father stood. Then she looked Jerry in the eye, swallowed and said, "Nothing."

"Nothing?" Jerry echoed.

"Yes, nothing." Her voice dropped to a whisper. "I'm sorry, Uncle Jerry."

Strauss saw shoulders coming down in the group. All except one who seemed unperturbed. He put his hand on the girl's shoulder.

"That's fine, Diana. Nothing is what you were supposed to hear."

"I don't get it," said Buck. "She obviously fell asleep. *This* is your big witness?"

"The curious incident of the dog in the night, Bradshaw," Strauss shot back. "Sherlock Holmes. The dog did nothing in the night and that was the curious incident. Diana heard nothing, *because there was nothing to hear*. And," he looked at each person in the room, "there is one person in this living room who knows exactly what that means."

Chapter 12: Keys

INGLESIDE 10:00 a.m.

He wasn't big, but he was fast.

The military training kicked in and Stan North grabbed Diana Wiley before anyone could move. He pulled her with him to the corner of the living room, backing into the gunslinger's corner to face them all.

And, inexplicably, Stan had a gun.

"No!" Wiley instinctively moved forward with Taylor on his heels, but Strauss put up a warning hand. The others moved back, Bradshaw quietly pulling Lynn behind him.

"Nobody move or the girl gets it," he said, putting Diana in front of him with one arm, while the other made a small pistol appear beside her head. "Isn't that the script? And you're right, Strauss. Staged is the word. I thought I put on a great show. The girl and I are going to quietly leave here with no trouble from you; but if you have a minute before I go, I'd like to know how you knew it was me."

Strauss looked at Diana. Her face was white but calm. She was her father's daughter, but he couldn't count on her nerves for too long like this.

Think.

"I pegged you right away, Stan," Strauss said firmly. Undermine the cockiness. "Your distractions were very entertaining, but the moment I stepped into the Brass Room, I had my eye on you."

"Why?"

"You were so busy with the details of your production that you missed one of the basics. Audrey's body is in the middle of the bed. If she were killed while sleeping in the middle, where the hell were you?"

"Shit." The gun came down an inch and Wiley took a step forward. "Do it again," said North, snapping the gun back up at Diana's head "and she doesn't graduate from high school."

Wiley put up his hands and stepped back. "Please," he said hoarsely, "let her go. She's just a kid. I'll go instead."

"No, thanks," Stan replied pleasantly. "A cop is just a suit. But a kid is a kid. Oh, I will take your guns, officers. Now."

Wiley and Taylor looked at Strauss. He nodded.

All three slowly took out their weapons and placed them on the living room floor.

"What about me?" Isabella spoke for the first time. "I'm a federal minister. I'm worth more as a hostage than a teenager."

"Are you serious?" North laughed. "Nobody likes politicians these days. No, I'm staying with the kid."

"The knife, Stan," said Strauss, straightening up. "It *is* the Granny Hoople knife that belonged to Daniel Sterling. Where did you get it?"

"Audrey, of course," the man explained. "She'd kept it all these years. Kind of like a trophy, I think. How did you figure out about the sleeping pills?"

"You had to have a reason for the two of you not waking if someone came into your room. You were military-trained," said Strauss. He shot a look at Wiley, whose face was a torture. The man would snap at any moment. Jerry had to hurry. "You would wake up on a dime if someone broke into your room, let alone killed your wife. So I figured the autopsy would eventually show high levels of some narcotic in Audrey's system. You also had to have traces in yours in case of a urinalysis. So you took some more after 'finding' Audrey's body, to make sure there would be some to find. That's why you were still so sleepy until now—but able to wake up at the crack of dawn to find your wife was murdered.

"I also found it odd that the phone line was cut in this house," Jerry continued, maintaining eye contact with Diana to keep her calm. "Seemed useless because it wouldn't slow anyone down this morning. Everyone has cell phones. Seemed dramatic. Seemed staged."

"Guess I've always had a secret flair for the dramatic," Stan smiled. "Well, this has been fun, but I better get going." North kept his arm around Diana while he made her stoop down to pick up the guns. He put them in his jacket pockets. "I want at least a half hour head start. No phone calls until then. Make sure of that, Sergeant."

And then it all happened very fast.

A young girl in a white dress broke through the group from the dining room and ran across to the hallway.

"What the—" Startled, North momentarily loosened his grip on Diana who instinctively pulled away from him.

"Di!" Wiley moved in to save her. There was the sound of a gun shot and he spun away, grabbing his shoulder.

"Daddy!" Diana screamed as Wiley hit the floor. Stan North pulled her back to him with a growl.

"Jordan." With a white face, Strauss knelt with Taylor over the man on the floor. It was a shoulder wound, blood seeping into Wiley's shirt from beneath his hand.

"Not me," Jordan whispered. "Diana, Jerry. Get Diana."

Someone started hammering on the front door.

"Strauss," came a muffled yell. "It's ten on the nose. You'd better have Isabella ready to go and no more bullshit."

Bella moved toward the front door.

"Leave it," said Stan curtly. "Let him cool his heels out front. The kid and I are going out back."

The man started toward the dining room, but Diana dug in her heels.

"I'm not leaving my dad like this." She started to squirm.

"Knock it off, kid, or I'll blow your brains out." North tightened his grip, but Diana fought harder.

"Strauss!" Again from the front door. "I'll give you to the count of three and then I'm going to fill this house with goddamn Mounties."

"Diana, no." Lynn stepped forward and put out a warning hand. Buck put his arm in front to stop her.

"*One*."

"Kid, I'm warning you." There was the sound of a click as North pulled back the trigger. Mildred covered her mouth with her hands.

"*Two*."

"Diana," Jerry stood up slowly. "Your dad's going to be fine. We have to stay calm."

Diana looked down at her father, her eyes filled with tears. "I'm sorry, Dad." She turned back to Strauss, opened her mouth to speak and then suddenly looked up over his shoulder, her body falling limp against North.

"*Three*."

The roar of a single shot tore through the room. For one moment, time and people froze, silent. Strauss opened his eyes and made himself look at Diana, hands out, waiting for her agony.

Then, in slow motion, the top of Stan North's head gave way, and he flew back against the wall, his blood spraying out behind him like a finger painting. With a silent scream, Diana dove to the floor beside her father. Bradshaw followed suit, pulling Lynn down with him.

There was fresh hammering on the door.

"Inspector! Sergeant Wiley!" came a new voice. "Open up!"

There was the sound of breaking glass as a pane was broken.

"My door!" Mildred yelled. She ran to the door, unlocked it and pulled it open, bringing in a wave of Matt Corning and ident officers that swirled in and broke around Jerry Strauss.

Wordlessly, they took in the scene before them.

"Inspector?" one asked.

"Strauss?" Corning bellowed. "What the hell . . . Bella? Are you all right?"

But Isabella ignored him. She stood by the davenport, one hand raised to point at the staircase in the front hall.

"There!" she said.

They all turned to look.

Hugh Keeps stood at the turn of the stairs, one eye still to the sight of an old rifle he held aimed at the living room. He did not move.

One of the ident officers drew his gun on the old man, backing around to the bottom of the stairs.

"Please put your weapon down slowly, sir," he said quietly, "and come down the stairs."

Hugh Keeps did not move.

Strauss came over and put out his hand. "Put your gun down, Constable. It isn't necessary."

The officer looked at Strauss, back up at Hugh, then slowly lowered his gun. One officer ran over to Wiley and Taylor, who was calling in the shooting. The others turned to Strauss expectantly.

Jerry moved quietly into the living room to look around, pausing at Stan's body in the far corner.

"We were all standing in the way," he said to himself. "He shot through us, through the columns of the divider wall, past a hysterical girl to one mark. Stan's head. And a dead hit."

Turning back, Strauss walked through the silent crowd to the bottom of the stairs and looked up.

"That was one shot in a million, Mr. Keeps," he said. "And in all my life, I've met only one man who could ever pull off something like that."

Strauss walked up several stairs to stand just below the old man.

"Daniel?" he asked gently.

Still the man did not move. He stood ramrod straight, no hat, glasses gone. He was breathing heavily, but the rifle didn't waver. For a few minutes, he did not speak. Then, finally, he slowly lowered the gun.

"I had to kill him," he said almost to himself. "He was going to kill the girl."

"I know, Daniel."

"But it doesn't seem right. He had the guts to do what I should have done years ago. He killed Audrey."

"'You can blast my other passions, but revenge remains,'" Strauss quoted. "'revenge, henceforth, dearer than light or food.'"

At that, the old man finally looked at Strauss and the years fell away. New face, older man, but the eyes had not changed. And they filled with tears.

"So you remember your Shelley, son," he whispered.

"Yes, Daniel," Jerry replied with a sad smile. "I've never forgotten. But I'm glad you didn't do it. You would have lowered yourself to her level. But this," Jerry indicated the gun, "this was right. This saved a life, maybe many." He shook his head and gently took the rifle from Daniel's hands. "We looked through this house and never saw this old gun. Where—"

Daniel chuckled and grinned that crooked grin.

"You forget, son. I grew up in this old house. She's got hiding places you'll *never* find."

Jerry stood on the stairs, rifle in one hand. He looked down at the faces below—Mildred, Buck, Lynn, Bella, Taylor, Wiley holding Diana with his good arm—and then at the mess of Stan North by the fireplace. He turned back to Daniel, took a step up to stand beside him and put his other hand on the old man's shoulder.

"Well," said Strauss simply, "let's thank God for that, then."

PART THREE

When your heart's retreating
From this lonely world
That's the time that you must stay
For it needs you
It needs you

—Ron Sexsmith, "I Know It Well"

Chapter 13: Home

INGLESIDE

"Paramedics are here, sir."

Jerry looked up at the officer from his seat next to Wiley on the davenport. Diana sat on the other side of her father.

"Good. Get them in here. This man needs a hospital."

Wiley stood up slowly.

"I can walk out, Inspector."

"Sit down," Strauss ordered. "You're in shock. You look like you're going to pass out."

Wiley wobbled, then obeyed. The paramedics came in with a gurney, and Strauss waved them over. When the sergeant rose again to get on the gurney, Strauss took his arm. Wiley stopped and turned to the man sitting silently in the chair in the corner.

"Mr. Sterling," he said, putting out his hand, "Thank you. Thank you for my daughter's life. My wife and I are forever in your debt."

The man looked up uncertainly. Then he stood to take Wiley's hand.

"You're welcome, boy," he said simply.

"Come on, Officer," said one of the paramedics. "We need to see to that wound before we can transport you. Let's get you out in the fresh air."

They guided Wiley onto the gurney and took it out through the front door. Diana and Strauss followed. Once out on the lawn, they went to work, Diana holding her father's hand.

"Strauss! What the hell is going on here? What's wrong with Sergeant Wiley? And where is Minister Roberts? She's supposed to be in the middle of press conference right now."

At the sound of the voice, Jerry turned to see Superintendent Holland materialized behind him like a bad genie. Christ. That's all he needed to round off the morning.

"Superintendent." Jerry forced what he hoped was a smile. "What are you doing here?"

"Checking up—checking in with you, Strauss. Didn't like the sound of things with your phone call. Thought I'd see if the minister needed anything."

"We're taking the body from the upstairs out now, Inspector." A crime unit officer came up behind Holland.

"The body?" said Holland.

"Take it out the back door, through the garage," said Strauss. "Let's not give the press and the gawkers any more than we need to."

"What body?" Holland looked at the retreating officer then back at Strauss. "What the hell is going on here?" he repeated.

"It's a long story, sir," said Strauss wearily. "About fifty years' worth."

"Strauss!" came another unwelcome voice. "I want to talk to you." Matt Corning came from somewhere within the crowd to face Jerry. "Or rather, I'm going to talk to your superior officer."

"That would be me," said Holland. "Who are you?"

"Matt Corning. Personal aide to Minister Roberts. I want you to know that—"

"That Inspector Strauss did an amazing job here today." Isabella Roberts came up to stand beside Jerry, facing Holland.

"Bella!" Corning fumed.

"Matt." She quelled him with a glance, then turned to Holland. "Your inspector had quite the situation on his hands this morning. And I made things worse by insisting on a blackout for a couple of hours to buy me time for the media conference. He accommodated me and used the time to solve the murder. Nothing short of amazing."

"Is this true, Strauss?" asked Holland.

"Not quite," said Jerry. "I had help. Sergeant Wiley and Constable Taylor did an excellent job here. Nobody works alone in this business."

"Minister Roberts?" Diana Wiley came up from where she was standing near her father.

"Yes, dear?" Bella turned to her. "How are you feeling after your ordeal? You must have been frightened to death."

Diana ignored the question, looked at her father and then back at the minister.

"Your plans for the Seaway Valley," she began hesitantly.

"Yes?"

"I think . . . I hope . . . I mean, well . . . Don't forget the children."

Bella looked puzzled.

"Bella, we have to go," Matt Corning interrupted. He pointed at his watch.

Isabella put up her hand. "The children?" she asked Diana.

"Yes," Diana said more firmly. "The children. Whatever funding or programs you're bringing here, make sure they include the children of the Seaway Valley. I mean, marketing and tourism are important, but so is the community. And the community will belong to the children someday." She thought for a moment, as though remembering. "They need a role, a voice," she continued. "They need to be involved in the history that's here and the history that's yet to come."

For a moment, no one said anything. Jerry looked at Diana, not a child anymore but capable young woman, yet just thirteen—the same age he'd been that summer in this house.

"I'll keep that in mind," Bella replied thoughtfully.

"One, two. Up." The paramedics hoisted Wiley into the ambulance. Diana moved to join him, then stopped. She ran back to give Jerry a hug. He held her tightly for a moment.

"Everything's going to be fine, now," he said gruffly. "Your mother's on her way to join you at the hospital. Off you go."

"Thank you, Uncle Jerry," she whispered. Then she climbed into the waiting vehicle, the doors closed and they were gone.

Jerry watched the ambulance pull away, thinking how close he'd come today to losing one of his best officers. And a friend. With the twenty years' difference between them, Jordan Wiley was young enough to be his son. They all seemed so young to him now—young, their whole lives ahead of them, out there, vulnerable. His officers. His family.

He suddenly remembered another young officer, a constable named Jerry Strauss, on a warm fall evening in 1968.

Constable Strauss drove down the old roads, heading for the river. With the flooding ten years before, the area had been left with myriad roads running to the water's edge. These dead ends were often used by teens and unsavoury characters, and the staff sergeant in Long Sault had a standing order for them to be checked regularly.

With great reluctance, Strauss had turned into the Migratory Bird Sanctuary and now headed where Aultsville used to be. Home, but home no longer. He came upon an old car sitting with its lights out beside the river. Parking, he walked up to the window to see an old man with clothes that spoke of farming.

"Is everything all right, sir?" the young man asked. He flashed his light into the interior of the car. It was empty of any contraband.

"Yep." The old man did not look at him, keeping his eyes focused on the river.

"May I see your driver's licence, please."

It was passed and returned.

Silence fell. Jerry nervously shifted his weight from one foot to the other. Then he cleared his throat.

"Just taking in the sunset, sir?"

At first, Jerry thought the man was going to ignore him. Then suddenly he spoke, in tones just above a whisper.

"My folks are buried out there," the old man said simply, eyes on the river.

For a moment, Strauss didn't know what to say. He hesitated to call it in. The staff sergeant wasn't from around here. He probably knew the history of the Seaway, but wouldn't understand how people felt.

Finally, the constable called it in. There was a moment's silence on the radio, then the staff answered.

"Leave him be," was the reply.

It had taken some people decades of their lives to come to terms with the upheaval and loss of the Seaway. For some, they never had.

"Inspector, may I have word with you before I go?" Bella's voice brought him back. Corning and Holland had moved off and were talking near the minister's waiting car. Jerry and Bella were alone for a moment. He looked at her thoughtfully.

"You want to know if I'll acknowledge our son?" he asked quietly.

"Yes."

"And he is our son?"

"I told you that." She waited.

"Answer me one question first, then," he said. "Will you ever stop using people, Bella?"

"What do you mean, Jerry?" Bella countered, poker-faced.

"You've lied to me several times this morning," Strauss explained. "It wasn't Bradshaw that was blackmailing you. It was Audrey. And Stan knew about it, too, which is why you were still nervous, even with Audrey dead. You not only lied about that, you were willing to implicate Bradshaw—use an innocent man to cover your ass."

She flushed. "That's business, not personal."

"The issue of my son is very personal, Bella. And very dirty pool. Even for you."

She looked at him, saw something in his eyes and turned away. Jerry stepped up close behind her.

"You're getting sloppy in your middle age, darling. Have you forgotten one of the reasons you left me? I was sick, remember? Had a brush with cancer, just like my mother. I was already in the first round of treatment when you left. The drugs would have made it impossible for me to father any child at that point. Another lie. And a monstrous one."

He took her shoulders and turned her to him. She looked him in the eye. He had to give her that much.

"Everyone is expendable to save the king, right, Bella? I guess you see children as fair game, too, to be set on the block for barter. Do you know where your son is?" He thought of Farran and her search for her daughter. "Are you even looking for him?"

At that, she turned her face away. So beautiful, so powerful, so much the one person to make him appreciate what he had in Farran Mackenzie. Mackenzie was neurotic maybe, loopy sometimes, but real. Always real.

"I'll help you if you need it," he continued. When Bella turned surprised eyes on him, Jerry shook his head. "Not just because I'm nice guy."

"There's a price tag," she said grimly.

"I'm just talking your language, Bella. Here's the deal. Fifty years ago, you people on Parliament Hill walked in here and did what you had to do. And the families here sacrificed what they valued the most. Fine. But then you left us standing at the altar for half a century. It's time to come back, to do it right."

"That's why I'm here this week, Jerry," said Bella. She turned to leave, but he grabbed her arm.

"This package you're announcing," he said, "is going to be done. It's going to be done right. And it's going to be done in a real partnership with this community, right?"

She didn't answer.

"In fact," he continued, "this initiative will be the biggest thing of your career. I will enjoy watching it take place," Jerry added pointedly. "And I will be watching."

Bella gave him a long look before turning to leave. Then she strode off to where Corning waited, got in the car without one backward look and was gone.

"Checkmate, love," Jerry said to himself.

Both Santa Cruz and Maxwell were blocked to through traffic. People now lined the barriers, trying to get a glimpse of the action. The media were beginning to gather, corralled on one side, listening to Superintendent Holland, shouting questions at him. Lynn and Buck were the exceptions, speaking with Constable Taylor. The crime unit officers moved in and out via the garage, the forensics van having taken the place of the "meat wagon" now gone with its first grisly cargo.

Strauss looked around wearily at the controlled chaos in the usually quiet village, suddenly feeling like lead from the neck down. He wanted to go home.

But first, one more thing.

Jerry turned to go into the house and stopped. Mildred Keeps stood on the front steps, Daniel Sterling on the sidewalk below, waiting.

"Daniel," Jerry whispered.

"Hello, son." The old/new face smiled hesitantly.

Mutability. Change. All men's decay. A river of time had swept through since Jerry had last stood by this house with this man. And yet, through the dual nature of perception, no time at all.

"I know why I would have killed Audrey," Daniel began. "But why did her husband do it?"

Jerry walked up the sidewalk to him.

"Just a guess for now, but Stan was addicted to gambling. Way in debt. Three months ago, he goes off the radar. Chances are that Audrey had cut him off and he wasn't willing to wait for her to die of natural causes to get the estate."

"Makes sense, I guess," Daniel nodded.

"How did you ever end up being Hugh Keeps?" Jerry shot a look at Mildred, who came down to take Daniel's arm.

"It was my idea," she said. "He did it to help me. It's not his fault."

"Now, Millie," Daniel protested.

"Daniel was living with my uncle in a seniors' facility. That's where we met."

"In Grimsby?" Strauss asked.

"Yes. About five years ago, my uncle died suddenly. I was alone and his pension was all we'd had to count on. I couldn't get work nursing anymore. I was too old." She looked up at Daniel. "He was alone, too. No pension, just the money he had in the bank that wasn't going to last forever. So I asked him to live with me, become Hugh Keeps. So Daniel Sterling died and Hugh

Keeps continued living. Daniel put his money into purchasing this house, and I kept my uncle's pension coming in."

"That's fraud," said Jerry. "No one suspected?"

"When you're old, son," Daniel answered quietly, "there's nothing easier than being invisible. It's like you don't matter anymore."

Jerry grunted in agreement.

"No, no." Daniel gave him a pointed look. "I mean *really* old— like me. Trust me, he added, "you're still a young man. You don't see it from where you're sitting. I do."

"So what now? You have to clear that up and you're in debt to the Norths." Jerry thought a moment. "The Norths are dead, and we could approach it as illegal gain with their estate."

"We?" Millie asked dubiously.

"We," Jerry replied firmly. "I'll help you sort this out. Make an honest woman out of you, Mildred Keeps." He smiled at the woman and could have sworn he got the ghost of a smile back.

"Did you realize who I was?" Daniel said.

"Things began to make me wonder," Jerry admitted. "So much of the house was done as it had been in Wales. Maybe Millie had found photographs and decorated it that way on purpose. Still, it was weird. The records said you were dead, and I accepted that. And Hugh Keeps did not have Daniel Sterling's damaged face. But looking at Matt Corning's manicured face this morning, I remembered there's a lot they can do now with plastic surgery that was impossible in the fifties."

Daniel ran a hand over his face. "It took time," he said. "It took several tries to get it this good. But they did it."

The small talk was done.

"Audrey killed Joe Beckett," Strauss said bluntly. "That's why she had the Granny Hoople knife and Stan was able to use it on her."

The old man nodded.

"And you knew she'd killed him, that summer."

No reply.

"And yet you confessed a week later to that murder and spent thirty years in jail." Strauss looked at his old friend. "Why?"

Daniel looked away.

Jerry put his hand on his shoulder. "Daniel," he persisted, "I think I've earned an answer to that question. Why would you take the rap for Audrey?"

For a moment, Daniel remained silent. Then he quietly replied, "Love."

"Love?" Jerry asked. "You still loved Audrey? She killed Joe, and you covered for her because you still loved her after all those years?"

"No," said Daniel, turning to face him. "You, son. Because I loved you."

Jerry shook his head. "You've lost me, Daniel. Why would you do it for me?"

"To save you from her. From Audrey." Daniel looked at the confusion in Jerry's face. "I first knew something was wrong the night you told me you'd seen Harriet's ghost. She only appears to children, they say, to protect them. I couldn't understand what the danger would be. But that night, I was looking at the will I'd made years ago, leaving everything to Audrey when I went to serve. I'd never changed it when she married Joe. I guess I just didn't care—about that or anything else. I lost myself after the accident. I felt as though the man I'd been had died in the war.

"Then, after all those years, you came. Into my house, into my life. Emme insisted, telling me it would be good for you. I think she knew it would be good for me, too. And it was. I started feeling alive again. Started to care again. I grew to love you as my own. You were quite the kid, son," he smiled. "It didn't take long." The smile faded. "Audrey sensed the change in me. She had animal instincts, that one. She'd already decided to kill Joe for his money and wanted to be sure she was still gettin' mine, to build a bigger house in the new town. I caught her goin' through my things one day when you were at the creek. I think she saw the notes I'd made for a new will, leavin' everything to you."

"Me?" said Jerry.

"Yes, you. And she set poor Joe up somehow to be in my house, maybe waitin' for some supposed tryst we were havin' when it was Buck's dad all along. She killed him with the knife, took it and the new will, then told me a couple of days later she would set you up for the murder if I didn't confess to it myself. That you had stabbed Joe, thinkin' it was me in the chair, wantin' the estate."

"That would never have held up in court, Daniel," Jerry protested.

"Maybe," said the old man. "Maybe not. I couldn't take the chance. And the trial would have been too much for you, son.

You were bleedin' enough as it was when I met you. I know a wounded soul when I see one."

"Daniel . . ." Strauss was speechless. He'd never seen it.

"But they didn't hang me after all," Daniel said cheerfully, 'and Audrey didn't get her inheritance. And that's what I meant about rememberin' your Shelley. In case you or your ma ever found out."

"'You can blast my other passions; but revenge remains—revenge, henceforth dearer than light or food!' From *Frankenstein*." Jerry nodded slowly. "I didn't get it until much later, when I was rereading the novel in high school. I remembered you and that night you gave me the book, and how we talked about Percy Shelley. I saw the poem you'd quoted about mutability in the novel and how the monster's favourite book was Milton's *Paradise Lost*—the other book you gave me that night. I realized that you had been trying to tell me something."

"That night it was just about what you'd lost up to then," said Daniel. "Your pa, your faith in a friend, your village, your sense of yourself. All those writers talked about the same thing—that life is a series of choices. Like with Frankl's book. How people chose to endure the horrors of the Holocaust. No matter what life throws at you, it is up to us to choose who we are. Free will. It's our divine right. I didn't want you to be bitter.

"Then Joe was killed and I had to go to jail. It seemed like another adult leavin' you in the lurch, I knew. So I told you to remember your Shelley. Revenge is a terrible poison."

"I thought you meant Percy Shelley," said Jerry, "but you meant the other Shelley. Mary Shelley."

They walked into the garden, Jerry leading Daniel to a chair under a tree. Daniel looked up at the old house, his eyes filling with tears.

"Audrey killed Joe," he said, "but putting the knife in his heart was only a token gesture. She'd killed his spirit long before. As I did."

"You?" Strauss stood in front of him. "What did you do? You were best friends."

"I killed his faith in me, someone he'd thought of as a brother his whole life." Daniel looked at Jerry. "That's why I understood how much the rumours about Hal Leonard killing your father hurt you."

"How could you possibly have done that?"

Daniel took in a deep breath and let it out. "We served together in the war. Summerside, P.E.I. Joe was there the night of my accident. His was the life I saved."

Strauss crossed his arms.

"So far, I don't see it."

"No," said Daniel simply. "No one knew. It was our secret. I could shoot weasels, son, but I couldn't kill. They taught me to fly those planes. To drop bombs. To kill from the air. It was war. The Nazis had to be stopped. But," he drew his hand across his eyes, "I knew I couldn't do it. I was a coward. Joe knew something was wrong, but had no idea what. We were days away from being sent overseas when he caught me one night getting ready to go AWOL. In one of the hangars. I was going to fly out. I guess I wasn't thinkin' straight.

"Anyway, Joe decided he was goin' to make me stay, even if he had to sit on me to do it. Needless to say, we got into a terrible fight and I knocked him cold under one of the planes. And ran like the coward I was. But we must have knocked over some gas cans, too. I wasn't two minutes out of there before someone yelled there was a fire in the hangar. I had to go back. No one knew he was there, or where. But I did. The whole front of the place was in flames, but I thought I was okay. Still had my flight suit on and my gloves. Forgot about my head. Ran in, wrapped him in a tarp and ran out. My hair was on fire and I passed out from the pain. Woke up in the infirmary with my whole head in gauze. They never understood why I didn't lose my sight, too."

Daniel fell silent for a full minute and Strauss waited.

"They gave me a goddamn medal for it," he continued finally. "For bravery. Joe made me take it. Said the truth would just kill my folks, and hurt everyone back home. So I did what he said. Cowardly again. Went home with my medal and no face, walked into that house, and never came out again."

They both looked at Sterling House, full of secrets, one now having been told.

"I came back from the war changed on the outside," said Daniel. "Joe came back later, changed on the inside. He spent a year in Europe, came home and married Audrey. He might have been okay if he'd had a wife with a heart. But she was the devil itself."

"You were ready to stand up for your beliefs. You walked into an inferno to save a life. And you went to jail to save . . . me."

For a moment, Jerry struggled to speak. "I have a friend, a good friend, who likes to call herself a coward, too. She's anything but." He thought of Farran since he'd met her—facing down three killers, hurling herself out of a burning building, running toward a bomb to save a life. "Why is it that the people who tell me they're cowards are the bravest people I know?"

"Uncle Hugh—Daniel." Mildred came over from the steps. "You should lie down now. You don't want to tire yourself too much."

"You heard the boss." Daniel rose with Jerry's help. "Coward or not, Millie scares the crap out of me."

Jerry laughed. "Good. I'm glad. That means she'll keep you in line."

"Speakin' of scary ladies, I saw you talkin' to the dragon lady before she left."

"Minister Roberts?"

"Yeah. Her. She givin' you a rough time over this morning?"

"Not that, but we did have an issue. Don't worry, Daniel. I sent her packing."

Daniel stopped to put a hand on Jerry's shoulder.

"I know you can't be bought, son. So if you can't be bought, be careful. That integrity can be a price in itself." He squeezed Jerry's shoulder and moved toward the porch.

"Daniel," Jerry called. "Can I come by now and then to see you? Catch up on things?"

"Of course." Daniel stopped and turned back. "Come over anytime. I'd like that. But," the crooked grin came back, "you don't need to tell me about your career. I've followed it all these years. So glad you chose to be someone who could make a difference—a police officer—instead of livin' bitter." The old man returned to Jerry, to put his hand back on his shoulder.

"I'll say now what your pa was robbed of sayin'," Daniel said, his voice growing husky. "I'm proud of you, son. We both are."

Strauss struggled for words again, but this time lost the fight. Wordlessly, he held Daniel close for a moment, then let him go.

The old man tousled Jerry's hair as though he were a child. "Taller than I remember," he joked, then walked over to the house.

"Welcome home, Daniel," Jerry whispered to himself. He watched the man slowly walk up and take Mildred's arm. They climbed the steps, entered the old house together and the door closed.

Boo Radley had come home.

"I'm going home, Taylor," he said, heading for his car. "I need sleep. You're first officer on the scene and it's yours until they send someone to replace Wiley. I'll make sure they get on it right away."

"Yes, sir." Taylor hurried after him and cut him off. "But I'm driving you home."

Strauss stopped and squinted at her.

"I beg your pardon?"

Taylor stood her ground.

"Sir, you haven't slept in almost a day. I really feel I should drive you home." She dangled the keys she'd taken from his car.

"Constable . . ."

"She's right, Jerry," Lynn called after him. "You're too whipped to drive. Let Margaret take you home."

"*I'd* let her take me home," Bradshaw grinned. Both Taylor and Lynn turned to give him a look.

"All right," Jerry relented. God, he was more tired than he could ever remember being. Just wanted to sleep for the next three days. "But, I want you to drive me to Long Sault. The detachment, not home."

Taylor opened her mouth to reply, then thought better of it. She crossed the street and held the passenger door open on her unmarked car.

Jerry made his way through the sea of people and got in.

"Guess the old man's had enough for one day," said Buck.

"That would be an understatement," Lynn replied dryly. "And he's not an old man."

"No, that wouldn't say much for us, would it?"

"No." Lynn looked around at the swarm of officers. "I don't know about you, but I'm out of here. The press conference is in half an hour. I guess I'll see you there."

She started to walk away.

"Hey, Lynn." Buck caught up with her. "About the banquet tonight. Are you going with anyone?"

"No. I'm just sitting at the press table, as usual. Why?"

Buck hesitated.

"I was wondering," he began, "if you'd like to go with me. Haven't seen you in a dog's age, and it would be nice to have some time to talk without . . ." he gestured behind him, "a murder investigation going on."

Lynn opened her mouth to say no, to make the standard excuses. But didn't.

"What's the matter, Buck?" she grinned. "Getting lonely in your old age?"

He crossed his arms.

"I'm never lonely," he said. "Just thought it would be fun."

She looked at him. So much water under the bridge, still so much the cocky boy he'd been in high school. Cocky, but not bad.

"It would be fun," she agreed. "Thanks, Buck. I'd like that very much."

"Stop here."

Taylor jumped at Strauss's request. They had driven in complete silence up till then and she'd assumed he'd quietly fallen asleep.

"Here, sir? The cemetery?"

"The cemetery, Taylor."

The constable slowed down and turned right off County Road 2 into the St. Lawrence Valley Union Cemetery, just opposite the Wales Road to the north. Strauss directed her around to the back section and they stopped beside the old remains of the original road into Wales.

"I'll be a minute." Strauss got out of the car and headed down one of the aisles until he reached a certain tombstone.

Emme Strauss
May 6, 1923
August 6, 1983
Beloved Mother

He stood looking at the stone for several minutes, hands in pockets. The sun began to make him drowsy.

"You didn't know, Ma," he said finally. "You didn't know what Daniel did for us."

Jerry remembered the last conversation he'd had with the woman he'd talked to his entire life. She'd been in the Ottawa General then, her body tiny and emaciated, her beautiful hair gone—victim of the chemo that had bought her only time, not life. She'd seemed more like a brittle doll than what was left of the strong, vibrant woman she had always been. But still, she'd managed to squeeze his hand.

"It's a choice, Jurgen," Emme had whispered with the last of her strength. Jerry had leaned in to hear her.

"What's a choice, Ma?" The morphine often made her ramble.

"Life. Life is a choice . . . It's that simple." She closed her eyes.

"I'll remember that, Ma," he said soothingly.

The eyes flew open.

"Love or fear, Jurgen." Emme's grasp grew strong in his. "Only two choices. Love or fear. Choose wisely." She closed her eyes again. "But choose."

She'd fallen asleep like that, later to slip into the coma from which she never returned. He had stayed with her, holding the hand that had always been held out to him.

"I'm choosing, Ma," Jerry said to the grave.

He'd chosen fear, not love, in believing Hal could have killed his father. Fear, not love, in not finding Daniel Sterling years ago. Fear, not love, in getting involved with Bella at all instead of looking for someone who was real. Now fear of not being up to the job anymore. And as for Farran Mackenzie . . .

"I'm choosing, Ma," Jerry said again.

He walked back down to the car, stopping for a minute to look out over the St. Lawrence River to the two islands behind the cemetery. They were the last remnants of the village of Wales, now out there under the water.

Then Jerry got back into the car.

"Take me home, Taylor."

She turned to look at him. "I thought you wanted to go to the detachment, sir."

"Same thing," he replied.

Wordlessly, Taylor started the engine.

The house stood in the middle of a storm—paramedics, police, press, crime unit van, and neighbourhood watchers.

I stood, taking it all in, looking for Diana safely wandering the yard behind the yellow tape. And for someone else. The source of all the mayhem.

You see, there is no greater force in the universe than an immovable object.

Strauss's usual procedure would be to hunker down, dig his heels in and wait until the players cracked under the pressure. But this had been different. This had been personal. And not only personal, but also something that touched a red button in Jerry's psyche. He had only one to my observation so far, but it was a doozy.

His father's suicide.

It was the revelation of this reality two years ago that took us from friends to lovers. And somehow, from what Lynn had told me earlier on the phone, I sensed that this house, the story inside that had begun half a century before, and the ending that had happened here today, were all connected to that open wound in the heart of Jerry Strauss.

I fingered a gold band that dangled from a chain around my neck—my father's wedding band, the ring they'd found on his skeleton in the mud flats of Aultsville almost four years ago.

"Fan!"

I turned at the nickname to see Lynn Holmes crossing the yard toward me. A tall man with curly grey hair followed behind, looking a little sheepish.

"Lynn." I gave her a hug.

"Glad you could make it to the party," she laughed.

"Did you find Diana?"

"Yes. She's safe and sound. Spent the night in a secret cubbyhole upstairs. She's gone in the ambulance with her father."

"Wiley? What happened?"

She put her hand on mine and squeezed it.

"He was shot in the skirmish, but in the shoulder," Lynn explained. "He's going to be fine."

"Quite the drama today," the man agreed.

"Oh, Farran," said Lynn. "This is my . . . my friend. Buck Bradshaw."

We shook hands. "The journalist?" I asked.

"Yep," he smiled. "But Lynn and I go back to the old days. My family was from Wales, and we both went to Osnabruck High right here."

"So you're actually a Seaway Valley boy?"

Buck hesitated. "Yes," he said finally. "I guess I am." He looked around the yard. "And this is going to make quite the story."

"It's my story," said Lynn.

"Why yours?" he protested. "You don't have copyright on it."

"I was involved," she shot back. "You were just a suspect."

"Just a suspect . . . ?"

I zoned out of the argument and scanned the controlled chaos again.

"Lynn," I interrupted. "Where is everybody?"

She turned from Bradshaw to me with a smile.

"Everybody? Well, let's see, Fan. If I'm not mistaken, Constable Taylor drove 'everybody' to the detachment. But wait a minute. We have to talk."

I squeezed her arm, ran to my car, and was gone.

When they reached the detachment in Long Sault, Taylor preceded the inspector up the front steps to open the glass doors for him. When she moved to follow him inside, he turned to give her The Look.

"Thank you, Constable," Strauss said not unkindly. "I can take it from here."

Taylor opened her mouth to reply, then turned away at the sound of a car in the parking lot.

Ignoring the probing eye of the receptionist from behind her cage window, Jerry crossed the lobby and headed down the long central corridor to his office. The place was quiet, with everyone still doing damage control on the 401 or security detail for the minister's tour.

Except for one figure at the far end of the hall. A civilian standing with arms crossed, head cocked to one side as he waited for Jerry to come up. A young man with fair hair and a lopsided grin Jerry would know anywhere.

He stopped dead in the middle of the hall.

"Hal?" Jerry whispered.

The young man nodded.

"Why . . ." Strauss began.

We'll always be friends, Jer . . .

Voices from the front lobby echoed down the hall toward Strauss. He felt a flicker of recognition and turned for a moment to listen, then turned back.

The hall was empty.

Jerry tried the doors to the stairwell and the other offices. All locked. Something deep within him was not surprised, and a feeling of peace accompanied that thought.

Fatigue finally overwhelmed him and he headed for his desk, falling heavily into the chair. The voices coming down the hall continued for minute, then stopped. Jerry wanted to stick his head out to see who it was, but that simple act was beyond him now.

Instead, he picked up a large brown envelope from the corner of his desk and contemplated its contents for a moment. His letter of resignation, his early retirement from the OPP. He'd drafted it last week and was waiting until the minister's tour was over before submitting it. It would, he knew, make Superintendent Holland's day. Hell, it would make his year.

Strauss thought of the day, the old house, the dying village of Wales in 1957, Mary Whitmore Hoople coming here as a stranger to her family after her own devastating loss to rebuild her life and save an entire community over two hundred years ago.

He thought of Daniel Sterling slowly walking up the steps to his house, leaning on Mildred's arm.

He thought of Diana Wiley running back to hug him before going with her wounded father in the ambulance.

If you can't be bought, son, be careful. That integrity can become a price in itself.

Strauss tore the envelope into little pieces, tossing them into the air with a tired smile.

"I don't think so, Holland," he said to the room. "This is my community. I won't give you the satisfaction. As Commander Montgomery Scott would say, 'Up your air shaft.'"

Jerry pulled a blank notepad toward him and grabbed a pen. Start the report. He leaned back in the chair, flipping the pen over and over on end, deep in thought.

Slowly the pen came to a halt.

Silence reigned.

Then suddenly, he knew there was someone at the door. With his last superhuman effort, Jerry opened his eyes.

Hal. It was Hal again, standing in the doorway, smiling that lopsided grin.

No. No, not Hal. Farran. Farran with dishevelled hair, crushed clothing and a coat hanging perilously from one shoulder. Farran with worry in her eyes—for him.

Farran Mackenzie was home.

His lids slammed shut, and he felt the pen slide out of his fingers to hit the floor. Footsteps made their way across the room to his desk. He felt her presence beside him, around him, inside him.

There was a slight rustle and something covered him like a blanket. Then the light brush of lips on his and again on his forehead with fingers softly in his hair.

"Now I *know* I'm dreaming," he muttered.

And then, Inspector Jerry Strauss truly slept.

I rested my head on his and held him until his rhythmic breathing told me he was out.

Love or fear.

Love is the only choice.

My heart was pounding, but I knew he was asleep. Bending to put my lips next to his ear, I made my mouth form the words I had not spoken to a man in almost a quarter of a century.

"I love you, Jerry Strauss."

There. It was said. I had made my choice.

"Are you ever going to tell him when he's awake?"

I jumped at the sound of the voice and straightened up to look into the twinkling eyes of Lynn Holmes, standing in the doorway, leaning on the frame with her arms crossed.

I flushed and fussed with the coat I had laid over Jerry's sleeping form.

"Say what?" I countered uselessly to my friend.

She grinned.

"It's okay, Fan. Your secret is safe with me. For now. And," she added, "for what my opinion's worth in this, the feeling is mutual. Now," she came over to Jerry's desk, "we need to talk."

"We should get him home," I said dubiously, looking at Jerry's somewhat sprawled position. "We can't let him sleep in this chair all day."

"That can wait a minute," Lynn insisted, coming around the desk to take my arm. "I have some news for you. You've led me a merry chase these past few days, and I've been wanting to tell you something. It's important."

She steered me to a nearby chair and sat me down.

I looked in her face but there was no clue as to gravity of the news.

"What is it, Lynn? Bad news or good news?"

She sighed and crossed her arms again.

"To be honest, I'd say both. The good news is that after all these months, I think we've found her."

I felt a rush of adrenaline go through me, making my heart pound and taking out my knees.

"Who?" I asked stupidly.

"Your daughter," Lynn said simply. "Haley. I think we've found Haley."

I felt both excited and scared to death. I suddenly also felt a little sick.

"And the bad news?" I clenched my teeth together to keep them from chattering.

"The bad news is that your instincts last year were right. If my information is correct, she's in trouble. In fact," Lynn's mouth became a grim line, "I'd say we've found her just in time."

Just north of Hoople's Bay, a short stretch of Hoople's Creek lives on, meandering through farm fields and under bridges as it has always done, making the journey to the bay it once did to the great St. Lawrence River.

The sun shone brightly on the little creek that afternoon as the children played on its banks, laughing, screaming and splashing in the warmth of the day.

A woman strolled among them, wearing a long dress and bonnet. Her face was timeless, her eyes filled with generations of wisdom and peace. A very young girl walked beside her, happily holding her hand.

"Granny! Granny Hoople!" A blonde girl in a white lace dress ran across the field toward them, waving her hands. Catching up, the girl threw her arms around the woman in breathless hug.

"Steady now, Harriet Sterling." The tone was stern, but the smile was soft. "What has happened, child?"

"I told her, Granny," said Harriet, looking up into the woman's face. "I told her everything you said to say. She listened."

The woman did not reply. Instead, she raised her eyes to follow the creek south to where it disappeared into the woods north of the bay.

"They are listening," Harriet said softly, as the woman put her hand on the girl's head. "It's begun."

"Granny," smiled Harriet Sterling, "the children are listening."

I hope tomorrow
Is clearer than today
Though in your house sorrow dwells
It never stays
I know it well

—Ron Sexsmith, "I Know It Well"

Appendix I

The Nightingale House Bed & Breakfast

The model for Sterling House and its history is one of the prettiest homes in the Seaway villages: The Nightingale House Bed & Breakfast. The house—the largest frame house to be moved to Ingleside during the Seaway construction—began its life in the Lost Village of Wales as the Warren-Rice home. Built in 1880, the house boasts butternut interior wood trim, original gas fixtures, and fireplace tiles from the pottery works formerly in the Lost Village of Mille Roches. It is a Victorian beauty, currently maintained to its period with antiques and art from that past age.

The house now stands proudly on its Ontario Hydro foundation in Ingleside, at the corner of Maxwell Avenue and Santa Cruz Drive. For many years, both in Wales and Ingleside, the Rice family ran an insurance agency from the home, serving the village and area. In 1999, the house was purchased by the current owners, Stuart and Lesley O'Gorman, who turned it into the popular bed and breakfast it now is.

Nightingale House is a unique inn, full of history and beauty. There is a large garden area to be explored and enjoyed, and afternoon Victorian teas to be savoured in the dining room. Harriet Sterling does not wander the halls, but Someone does— Someone, the O'Gormans say, who is discreet and beneficent.

Stuart and Lesley are excellent hosts as well as my good friends, and I have so enjoyed capturing the essence of their lovely home in these pages. (Sorry, I had to make the owner a widow, Stu . . .).

"I must add that while Lesley O'Gorman is petite and British and an avid gardner, at the writing of this novel she did not own pink mules. However, due to reader interest and participation, Lesley is now owner of a growing collection of this distinctive footwear. Also, to my personal knowledge, the O'Gormans have never found a guest dead in bed—yet."

Appendix II

Mary Whitmore Hoople (1767-1858)

The story of Mary "Granny" Hoople contained in this novel is true. She is an amazing part of the history of the Seaway Valley and its people.

In the spring of 1780, Mary's family was massacred on their farm on the Pennsylvania frontier by Revolutionary Indians, with only five children surviving. Mary was separated from two of her siblings, and carried off on horseback with her older sister Sarah and younger brother John. Over time, both Sarah and John were taken away and Mary was raised by a Delaware medicine woman she called Mother Medicine. For seven years, she lived the life of a native, learning the crafts of healing and herbal medicine that would serve her so well later in life.

In 1787, Mary was sold to the British for food for her starving tribe and she began the long journey home. Her nearest relative was her mother's brother, Jacob Sheets of the Longue Sault Rapids—a settlement that became the Lost Villages of Dickinson's Landing and Wales. Mary arrived a young woman ' who spoke no English or German to find a community desperate for food. She taught her new family and neighbours how to find food in the forest and later used her skills to minister to the sick. She quickly became known simply as the "doctor woman."

Mary fell in love with Henry Hoople. They married and had twelve children, raising eleven to adulthood. Mary lived to the ripe old age of ninety-one, still practising folk medicine and fondly referred to as Granny Hoople.

The tombstones of Henry and Mary were moved during the Seaway construction and can be found in the Pioneer Memorial at Upper Canada Village in Morrisburg, Ontario. The Hoople home still stands on the Second Concession of what is now the Township of South Stormont.

The Granny Hoople knife that belonged to Daniel Sterling is a creation of mine. No such knife exists. However, we do have one artifact from the life of Mary Whitmore Hoople. There is a china bowl with a floral design, cracked and darkened by age, that Mary used to carry balm of Gilead salve in her saddle bags when ministering to the sick. That bowl may be seen at the Cornwall Community Museum in Cornwall, Ontario.

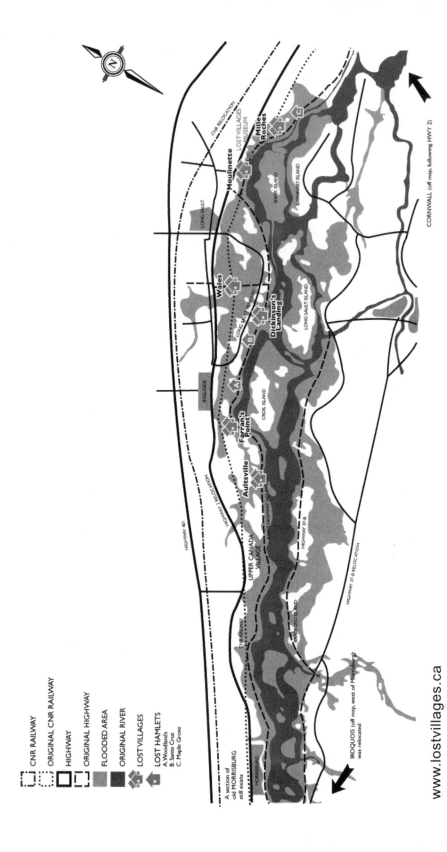

www.lostvillages.ca

Appendix III

The Moccasin

The author will defer this section to Rosemary Rutley, whose description of the village train, the Moccasin, in her book, Voices from the Lost Villages, *says it best.*

A most vital part of rural life, as essential to the Villagers as the St. Lawrence River, was the Railway. Several trains passed by the Villages but by far the favourite was the steam engine which travelled daily from Brockville to Montreal. It carried milk and mail and other cargo back and forth to points between the two destinations. It was fondly called "The Moccasin" named after the moccasined Indians from nearby islands who travelled on it. Some travelled it collecting hickory wood and reeds for their axe handles and handwoven baskets, while others used it to get upriver to catch the rafts which they would ride down the Longue Sault Rapids to Montreal. The Moccasin brought Village students to and from high school and college in Cornwall. Other passengers would take their lunch and spend the day shopping in Montreal or Cornwall. At Christmastime many went just to enjoy the Christmas lights in the store windows. Families would leave their supper tables and run to the Railway Station each evening to watch the old Moccasin come in. For many that was the day's main event.

The Moccasin ran the Montreal–Brockville route for one hundred and three years. But express trucks and other more modern transportation stole her trade and on August 9, 1958, the magnificent train made her final run, her steam whistle cutting the silence of the Lost Villages already under water.

Rosemary Rutley
Voices from the Lost Villages

Contributors and Resources

Aubin, Romeo. Formerly of Wales. Interview with author, fall 2004.

Brooks, Melanie. "Canada's Ghostbusters on the Prowl," *The Ottawa Citizen.* Ottawa: July 14, 2001.

Hoople, Elizabeth. *The Hooples of Hooples Creek.* Toronto: Ryerson Press, 1967.

Hoople, Elizabeth. *Medicine Maid: The Life Story of a Canadian Pioneer.* Belleville: Mika Publishing Company, 1977.

Laflamme, Fran. Formerly of Wales. Interview with author, summer 1999.

Marin, Clive and Frances. *Stormont, Dundas and Glengarry: 1945–1978.* Belleville: Mika Publishing Company, 1982.

O'Gorman, Stuart and Lesley. Owners of the Nightingale House Bed & Breakfast. Ongoing interviews, questions and other forms of friendly harassment from the author, 2004–06.

Rice, Eric. Formerly of Wales. Last of the Rice family to own the Rice-Warren house / Nightingale Bed & Breakfast. Interview with author, March 2005.

Rutley, Rosemary. *Voices From the Lost Villages.* Ingleside: Old Crone Publishing and Communications, 1998.

Stuart, Donald. *No Roads Back: A Grown Boy's Stories of Wales.* Ingleside: Old Crone Publishing and Communications, 1999.

Thank you to Jim Brownell, MPP for Stormont, Dundas and Charlottenburgh, for lending me the Hoople books that are now, sadly, out of print.

A special thank you to Ron Sexsmith for letting me use his wonderful songs within the pages of this book.

And to the Cool Chicks of South Stormont and Beyond: You offered true friendship, tough love and technical support when life began to change. Without you, this book would never have been completed. The Chicklettes and I—and the Beag—will be forever grateful.

About the Author

Born in Simcoe, Ontario, Maggie Wheeler moved with her family several times before settling in Long Sault. Much of her childhood was spent there in the former Hydro Town Site No. 2, one of two new towns created to accommodate villagers relocated by the St. Lawrence Seaway and Power Project.

With her roots now deep in eastern Ontario she still makes her home on the river at Ingleside—Seaway Town Site No. 1—in a house that once stood at the Lost Village of Dickinson's Landing.

Steeped in the Lost Villages, Maggie continues her journey to explore the emotional and cultural cost of the St. Lawrence Seaway. That is, when she is not melding the mystery genre with her passion for Canadian history.

www.maggiewheeler.com